D1045198

ALSO BY KAROLINA WACLAWIAK

How to Get into the Twin Palms

The Invaders

Life Events

Life

Events

KAROLINA WACLAWIAK

FARRAR, STRAUS AND GIROUX
NEW YORK

Farrar, Straus and Giroux
120 Broadway, New York 10271

Printed in the United States of America
First edition, 2020

Library of Congress Cataloging-in-Publication Data
Names: Waclawiak, Karolina, 1979– author.
Title: Life events / Karolina Waclawiak.
Description: First edition. | New York : Farrar, Straus and Giroux, 2020.
Identifiers: LCCN 2019056427 | ISBN 9780374186951 (hardcover)
Classification: LCC PS3623.A284 L54 2020 | DDC 813/.6—dc23
LC record available at https://lccn.loc.gov/2019056427

Designed by Gretchen Achilles

www.fsgbooks.com
www.twitter.com/fsgbooks • www.facebook.com/fsgbooks

1 3 5 7 9 10 8 6 4 2

For Robyn O'Neil

THE PEOPLE YOU LOVE
BECOME GHOSTS INSIDE
OF YOU AND LIKE THIS
YOU KEEP THEM ALIVE

—Robert Montgomery,
People You Love, 2010

Life Events

1.

The hills around the freeway were a dusty yellow, showing wear from months of drought. Winter rain hadn't settled in yet, and the last few years had been absent any significant storms.

I was not good at having confrontations, so I was fleeing again.

After you've driven through Mojave, California, there isn't much left in the way of towns as you head north. An airplane graveyard sparks up from the dry brush a few miles out, where pickup trucks with DON'T TREAD ON ME stickers drive fast on narrow roads. The kind of roads that lead into vast desert nothingness, punctuated only by rusted, spray-painted freight trains that roll slowly toward one border or another.

Outside Mojave, red rocks spring up before giving back over to flat, dusty land dotted with wind-worn white crosses jutting out at different mile markers by the road, signifying people who didn't make it home.

This emptiness, of places long past their boom—mining towns and turn-of-the-century company towns—felt comfortable to me. I looked for burned-out ghost towns next to long-shuttered convenience stores, because I liked to think about the limitations of what someone's imagination could build out here.

I stopped at one such relic on my drive, enticed by a sign that looked newer than anything else alongside the road, announcing FROG BALLS FOR SALE. The store's glass doors were grimy and locked, the shelves dusty and half filled with faded boxes of Hamburger Helper and milky-hazed jars of what I could only assume were floating frog balls. This ghost town was not all that different from other roadside stops I had made before—it was just missing a burned-out Cadillac out front. Here, freestanding motel bungalows with broken-down doors lined the two-lane road, evidence of a simpler time. One such bungalow had been converted into a bar with a rotting piano inside, with bottles strewn across tables and yellowed American flags serving as both window dressing and curtains to diffuse the light. It was the kind of place that looked like bad things happened there—both when it was up and running, and now.

"Evelyn was not a mistake."

I repeated this a few times as I walked through the bungalows. Each time, I changed how I emphasized my name. I tried the sentence as a question, too, wondering if a question mark had ever been considered instead of a period. It was a sentence my husband, Bobby, had written on the third page of his journal. I don't know why I picked it up and flipped through it, but I wasn't sorry.

Route 395 along the Eastern Sierras is my favorite drive in California, because it is both desolate and alive with people looking for an exit from their lives. I had done it before—alone and not—a number of times and was always charmed by the seeming lawlessness of this stretch of California. On the open road I never saw highway patrol or police of any kind, and I could drive well over the limit until I hit a speed-trap town, where I'd go from ninety to thirty-five before I reached the first stoplight or a lumbering RV slowing things down as the road narrowed from highway to Main Street every forty miles or so.

I always found someone to pace with on my drive—usually a pickup truck or some other loner to align myself with. I wondered where they were going and made up stories about a soldier just home or a rancher heading to his land. Always men, because men always seemed to be going somewhere alone. The women I saw were part of family units: passengers in SUVs or drivers for packs of sporty children. I didn't often see women like me—women heading to an unknown destination, alone.

On my drive this time, near the turnoff to a gas station, a motorcyclist entered the highway. I could tell immediately it was a woman, the way her leather jacket clung to her slim frame. She and I drove side by side for miles and I made up stories about her: tried to answer what might be in the small pack she had tied at the back of the bike, what color her hair was under her helmet, if we were close in age or not. And where she was going and if there was anything stopping her from riding away from her life forever.

When cars slowed her down, I let her slide in front of me. On the road, as we paced each other, she became my ideal, the kind of person I wanted to be. And before she turned off to the road that led to Death Valley, she looked at me and nodded. My heart soared at this acknowledgment. I slowed to watch her become a black speck disappearing on the horizon and imagined that one day I would be able to find freedom, too.

My phone rang, and I looked at the console to see Bobby's name. I considered not picking up, but after three rings I punched Accept.

"Did you see my texts?"

I looked down at my phone and saw I had missed six.

"They're not coming through for some reason."

"I don't know why that keeps happening. You need to get your phone checked."

"I should."

"What time are you leaving work?"

"I have to stay late. A few more hours at least," I said.

"Maybe pick up something for us to eat before you do?"

"Like what—"

"Just get whatever."

He hung up before I could say anything else. I looked in the rearview. No one was behind me, so I slowed to pull a U-turn and reluctantly headed back to Los Angeles.

2.

I stopped at the grocery store in our neighborhood before I got home, charging the credit card we shared to conserve the money I had in my own account. I didn't want to tell Bobby that I was no longer employed, because I didn't want the questions—did I get laid off, did I get fired, was I being impulsive again. Instead, I kept quiet and found places to go during work hours. My former employer was nice enough to give me six weeks of severance, even though I was pretty sure I didn't deserve it. He liked me. I liked him. It was a no-fault situation. That's what I told myself, anyway. I sent a thank-you note, because I was nothing if not thoughtful and I wanted him to think I was a good person. I was squirreling away as much severance as I could into my meager savings account—for the future.

When I got home, Bobby wasn't in our apartment, but I assumed he'd be back soon, so I got to cooking. I made an entire meal and ate it, and he still did not come home. I went to sit on our patio to have a drink, and then another—not to wait for him exactly, and not to get drunk exactly.

Sitting on the patio, taking frequent sips from my glass, I noticed a small bird body quivering in the dusk light. I put my glass down and leaned over to get a closer look. His feet were curled around the rim of my hummingbird feeder, and his small, feathered body convulsed, eyes closed, tongue lurching in and out of his beak.

I hadn't expected to spend my evening watching a hummingbird die. But I didn't know he was dying just then. I thought he might have been sleeping, or, foolishly, I thought he was just resting.

There's a woman to call when you find a hummingbird in distress. I dialed her number while staring at the bird as he swayed forward and back. When I explained the symptoms, and the sway, she told me the bird was dying. She said it was experiencing an excruciating death. She said I could help it along to ease its suffering.

I found a box and a hand-towel and made a bed for him. I cupped my hands around his tiny bird body and was surprised that his feet would not move. I tried to pull at him again, gently, and finally the bird gave in to me. I laid him down on the towel, tucked him in, and took him inside. It was one thing to feed a bird and another to become responsible for its life, or snuffing it out.

Outside, in the dusk light, the hummingbird's feathers were a dirty brown, but inside each feather shimmered a brilliant magenta and teal. I tried to quantify the size of each feather, anticipating one day telling the story at a dinner party of how I played death doula to a bird, and couldn't find an appropriate equivalent. Smaller than a snowflake? What would sound good in the retelling? Why had I immediately assumed it to be "he"? I had read that male birds always had superior plumage to females, in order to attract. Males held the power and the beauty.

The name of the woman on the phone was Helen, and I kept saying things like "That's terrible to hear, Helen," and "Are you sure he won't survive, Helen?" and "Oh, that sounds awful, Helen." I wondered if she thought I had made the bird sick—if she was silently judging me during the call. I worried that I was the cause of his suffering. Helen told me if I was calling her I cared enough to have not been the cause.

She hoped that I cared enough to kill it.

Helen told me to crush up an anti-inflammatory pill and mix it with the simple syrup I made each day for the mass of hummingbirds that would migrate to our feeders. She said to mix in one crushed tablet of my anxiety medication, to let the hummingbird go to sleep. She told me it would be okay, that doing this would not make me a bad person. To make me feel better, she kept saying it was going to die anyway. I found my bottle of Xanax at the bottom of my purse, took one myself, and broke another half pill to crush up and mix with the syrup. I found an eyedropper and took all the steps Helen advised.

The bird did not die right away.

I spent hours with him, dropping the mixture onto his tongue, hoping he would take the sip that would finally dull his pain. The agony was in the waiting. At one point, his feathers stopped shivering with iridescent light. His eyes opened and I hoped he saw me trying to help. I refilled the dropper over and over and finally watched the bird lie down on his side, tucked into the seams of the towel, and breathe easier. Convulse less.

In the aftermath, all I felt was a kind of blankness. I buried him in one of our potted plants on the patio, in the shadow of a succulent.

3.

A few weeks after the hummingbird's death, I sat in a dingy conference room, staring at the backs of strangers. Grieving strangers. When I had originally searched for grief support groups online, what came up were twelve-step programs, ranging from ones that helped people who loved too much to ones for people who couldn't find a way to love at all. Programs for people who looked for things outside of themselves to save them, or to obliterate them. And then I found this.

I had become exhausted by a kind of grief over the last few months, surprised by the physicality of it; prone to naps after reading e-mails from my parents about necessary visits that I could not bring myself to respond to. I could spend weekend hours catatonic in bed, staring at the wall. I tried to imagine what I could place directly across from where I slept so I could be calmed back to sleep instead of overcome by dread.

Every night I would open my eyes and listen to the night birds calling to each other, then gently slide out of bed to sit on the couch and watch hours of TV on mute while googling whatever popped into my head. The mockingbirds singing outside my window were the soundtrack to my insomnia.

One night, I found myself googling how long it took for

hummingbird bodies to decompose, which led me to forums about the afterlife and websites devoted to practical advice for living life and facing death, and, finally, a training program that taught people how to help other people die.

We would serve as exit guides for the dying. I had no idea such a job existed.

As I filled out the application, I was startled to hear the unfamiliar drip of rain outside. I walked to the window to see the first rain of the year and wondered how I could have forgotten what something so ordinary sounded like.

Bobby never stirred when I crawled out of bed. We were no longer the type to be tangled up together at night. At that hour, channels were flooded with infomercials for "As Seen on TV" gadgets to improve your life and give you optimal health. Men with bulging muscles in too-tight shirts pressed Liquefy on blenders full of "superfoods" and immunity boosters on a loop every night. They crammed kale and carrots into juicers and stuck their fingers in the froth to illustrate how absolutely no nutrients were lost before pouring the liquid into their mouths.

While I watched, I took hits of my weed pen and tried to will myself to sleep. I also often contemplated opening another bottle of wine to chase the one I had inevitably finished at dinner—but I was anxious that the recycling bin might look concerning. I often just took a Xanax instead. No one was counting my pills except my doctor. She had suggested the weed pen because she was less worried about my becoming a stoner than my developing a dependency on benzodiazepines. I decided that together they would be most effective to usher me back to bed, so each night I played with dosages in hopes of finding the right mix. So far I was up to 1.5 milligrams of Xanax and three hits of the highest-THC pen I could find. But I was still running on two or three hours of sleep, max, or what people call fumes. I found it was hard to get up in the morning after sinking into my pillow. I would usually spend ten minutes determining if I was still high (answer often yes) before finally pulling myself up and into a too-hot shower to sober up.

When my insomnia had become unmanageable, my attempts to avoid grief had finally placed me exactly where I needed to be: among people struggling with their own sorrows—whether it be about humans, dogs, or a cat now gone—who wanted to do something about it.

In the session, I sat across from a young man crying about how he had lost his father in 9/11—a first responder—and his stepfather had left him and his mother, so she had decided to focus all her attention on drinking. Andrew said he wanted to prepare for her inevitable death, which was why he was here. He was tough, he said. He had been through a lot. Everyone made sure to remind him of that every time they looked at him. He had moved to L.A. to get away from people who knew his story—and the looks they gave him. He was a survivor, but didn't want to feel that way all the time. But what he broke down about was not the eventuality of his mother's dying, but that his girlfriend had slept with someone else. She wasn't supposed to leave him, and yet she did. He said he thought they had made an unspoken pact: he would take care of her pain and she would take care of his. In leaving, she had become another variable in his compounding grief.

"There must be something wrong with me," he said. "I must be radioactive to be around."

We nodded because we understood. The leader of the training program was named Bethanny, and she was somewhere in her fifties. She wore a long flowing skirt and had silver hair tied in the kind of braid that cascaded over her shoulder and down the front of her blouse. She asked us to give space to Andrew's grief. There are so few places to allow for breakdowns or other kinds of outbursts of emotion, Bethanny said. She wanted this space to be one of them.

Displays of vulnerability by others made me anxious and even a little bit disgusted. In some ways, it felt like whatever these people were going through could be managed and they were just bad at managing it. I didn't like to see anyone's weakness and worked hard never to show my own. Even here, where we were supposed to feel free to be sad without judgment.

We held space for Andrew, who was no more than twenty-four. I did, too. He stared at me while he talked about the terrible things his girlfriend did to him. About how he felt like a man who was pegged as a victim from the very beginning of his life.

I wanted to have sex with him so he could feel better. The way I looked at him felt hungry, and I thought he could see that in me. I wanted to take his pain away, obliterate it through momentary pleasure. I wanted to tell him he could transfer his pain to me because I could endure it. I could endure anything.

People were speaking freely here, often through tears, about the weight of their loss and the opportunities they had missed to tell their loved ones how important they were. So instead they told us. And here I was, joined in mourning with people I had never met before. About a marriage to someone who did not know what was coming his way, and the inevitability of my own parents' passing. I observed the grieving. I thought it would help me sleep. If I'm being honest, I had been in rooms like this before—ones that housed support groups, which worked for me until they didn't.

But this room was different. This was job training.

Bethanny said she was deeply committed to helping people die consciously and to creating an army of empaths who could be sent out into the world to spread the word of death acceptance. We were doers. We were performing a service, and she had chosen us through our carefully filled-out applications. She said she could tell that there were some applicants who were not in it for the right reasons and so they didn't make the cut. We were handpicked to perform this service for others. She wanted us to know we were special.

But before we were sent out in the field as exit guides, there were a number of self-assessments we had to get through. The first was an exercise that we used to prepare ourselves for death, which Bethanny said required the kind of relationship to truth and honesty that most people do not have. We paired up, seats facing each other, and held hands. Nathan was sitting two seats away from me and introduced himself as he swiveled his seat around and faced his palms out toward me. "How are you?" he asked. The truth was, and always is, that I didn't know. But I mouthed "fine" with a smile so we could move on.

Bethanny wanted Nathan in here as a support for the new trainees. He told me he had already been out in the field and said it was "heavy but meaningful work."

Nathan had crow's-feet around his blue eyes and he looked of indeterminate age—maybe thirty-five, more likely a healthy Los Angeles forty-five. He wore New Balance sneakers, a dark-blue T-shirt, and unfashionable jeans that he probably thought were fashionable. He was a person you would pass on the street and maybe casually stare at for too long, but not in a way that made you feel hungry for someone. He was the kind of person you could project whatever you wanted onto.

Bethanny called out, "Look down at your sheets of paper.

You'll ask the question to your partner over the course of five minutes. Then you'll switch."

I looked down at the sheet of paper and there was only one question on it: "How do you avoid pain?"

We were about to launch into what Bethanny called "pain-avoidance techniques" with each other, and all I wanted to do was escape. Nathan seemed to be a joiner, whereas I was not. I had watched as he walked up to people at the beginning of the session and introduced himself to strangers like they were friends he couldn't wait to have. He seemed to be able to produce a casual intimacy with anyone. I wanted that sort of ease, too, but instead I was the kind of person who avoided eye contact.

"Do you want to ask first or should I?" he said. "Evelyn, right?"

In the sea of names, he remembered mine. The gesture felt meaningful to me.

"You," I said, and instantly regretted it.

He smiled and said, "How do you avoid pain, Evelyn?"

"Xanax. Sometimes Klonopin instead."

He was unfazed. I was starting off easy.

"How do you avoid pain, Evelyn?"

"Wine."

"How do you avoid pain?"

"My weed pen."

"How do you avoid pain?"

"Obviously, however I can."

I had run out of the kind of answers that felt safe to disclose, so I was moving on to jokes. He asked me again and I said, "Making jokes."

People were echoing the question all around us, but I

couldn't make out their murmured answers. The question itself had taken on the quality of an incantation vibrating through the room, and I suspected it was supposed to lead us to transcendence, but I wasn't feeling it.

Nathan settled into his seat and asked me again. We had four and a half minutes to go.

"Sex," I said. It was mostly a lie now. I wanted to see a reaction, but again I got none. Why did I want to get a rise out of him? I wasn't prone to acting out anymore.

"How do you avoid pain?"

"I don't know."

"How do you avoid pain, Evelyn?"

I didn't feel pain anymore.

"I avoid people," I said.

"How do you avoid pain?"

"I avoid relationships. Relationships are for other people," I said, smiling.

It didn't feel true, but I wanted it to be.

"How do you avoid pain?"

"I shut down."

I was shutting down. The question was floating all around me and I was starting to feel light-headed—as if I was on the verge of an anxiety attack. My face felt hot, and I wondered if he could tell that I was melting down or if I was hiding my spiral well enough to go unnoticed. He stared at me. Had I broken something in him? I hoped so.

"Evelyn, how do you avoid pain?"

I searched the walls for a clock but found none. Five minutes felt like an eternity when you were in an endless loop of defending yourself. I looked around and saw people crying. They were transcending their own humanity or something, having breakthroughs. But I had given Nathan a bum deal. He would not break me.

"I don't feel pain."

"What?"

"All I feel is pain."

"Time!" Bethanny shouted as a headache began to sprout behind my eyes.

Nathan said, "Great answers. Loved them. So good."

He could not stop smiling at me and patted my knee, and even reached to squeeze my hand. I did not stop him. The palm of his hand felt rough against my skin, and I imagined what he did with his hands to make them feel so rough. As he looked at me, proud that we had shared a moment, I could feel that I had sweated through the back of my shirt. I looked at the people comforting their partners and could tell everyone around me had reached a new level of understanding. But I didn't feel closer to Nathan. I gave him a weak smile back, feeling like a fraud who couldn't transcend anything.

"Switch," Bethanny called out.

I stared at Nathan and I could tell he was excited for this.

"How do you avoid pain, Nathan?"

"I run," he said.

"How do you avoid pain?"

"I really listen to what a person is saying when I'm with them. Really give them their space to feel their feelings, you know what I mean?"

I nodded and said, "Uh-huh."

4.

After the first exit-guide training with Bethanny, I was completely exhausted. I told Bobby I wasn't feeling well and crawled into bed without eating dinner. I fell asleep without weed or Xanax, and I had a recurring dream, one that I hadn't had in a few weeks. It was the kind that scared me into believing that I can see the future. And it always started the same way.

In my dream, my mother and father are staying with me and I am afraid my father will die and I don't know what to do with the body.

I need to get my parents from Point A to Point B, where I live to where they live, in the middle of the Southwest. My father is starting to wane—he looks twenty years older than his age, beat up from wearing himself down, in pain all over his body. An oxygen machine assists my mother's breathing, and she believes she will die without it. I help my father with the crutches he is using, and we set out into the L.A. traffic, pointed toward the desert. In my dream, I am in the car with these dying people and I am tasked with making sure they make it out of here alive.

We don't speak for the first seventy or so miles, until we

reach the wind turbines that dot the parched hills cascading toward signs for Palm Springs.

"They're ugly," my mother murmurs, staring out the window as the small portable oxygen machine we have plugged into the car lighter clicks and wheezes like she does when she breathes.

"I like them," I say. And we have already found a divide. I look at my father in the rearview mirror to find an ally, but he only stares out the window at the sea of white turbines with his vacant eyes and doesn't say a word.

We are running against time in this car, but we still need to eat, so we stop at McDonald's to get Egg McMuffins, and we quietly chew while I drive. We hardly speak, because what is there to say? Instead, we take turns using my mother's new fingertip oxygen tester on each other, to test the amount of oxygen in our blood. I don't know how it works, but it does. My mother tests herself first. Without oxygen pumping into her nose through a clear plastic tube, she only has 78 percent oxygen in her blood. This is bad. This is why we presume she is dying. The normal amount of oxygen in your blood should not dip below 88 percent. She asks my father for his fingertip and he produces it between our seats and she clicks the tester onto his finger and we wait. When his reading says 96 percent she feels like she's lost something, a competition, but they have different ailments, so it's hard to compare.

"Let's test the healthy one," my mother says.

"I'm driving," I say.

"Just give me your finger."

I do what she tells me to do, because she is my mother, and when my reading comes back 100 percent she says, "Do you see this? She's perfect."

But the problem is, I'm not, and I know it.

We whiz past exits and rest stops into the open desert, where there are whirling dust devils on either side of us. Some are small and some look like massive tornadoes of dirt. One crosses over the road we are driving on and I wait for something miraculous to happen, but it just disappears around us.

"We should be taking care of you, not the other way around," my father says from the back seat. I take note but stay silent. He does this now: makes unprompted declarations laced with guilt.

Ahead I see the dark clouds of thunderstorms and watch as soundless lightning shoots down into the nearby hills. I know we are going to drive into the storm, and my mother is scared, but I tell her not to worry. When we reach the rain, it is torrential and I can't see the yellow lanes anymore, but I can't just announce that, so I keep quiet. My father is frozen in silence in the back seat, still staring out the window. Lightning strikes near his side of the car, but he doesn't jump, he just opens his mouth in childlike awe. As we reach the edge of the clouds, I slow the windshield wipers and open the window to smell the rain on the hot asphalt.

From the back seat my father says, "Petrichor."

"What?" my mother asks.

"That's what this smell is called," he says as the sun envelops us.

"I didn't know," I say, watching him nod in the rearview mirror. I worry I will never know half of what they know and there isn't enough time to ask.

We don't stop driving until we reach Tombstone, Arizona, and by then the sun is setting and the sky is a kind of pink I've never seen before in real life. I've driven through the Southwest dozens of times and have seen the desert skies alight with the sunset before, but in my dream the sky is the color of sherbet, because the sun is setting behind storm clouds. It feels hopeful, even though things inside the car are dire. The three of us are looking for any kind of hope, so when I stop at the rest stop to go to the bathroom, I roll down the windows and yell, "Look!"

My father is preoccupied with his crutches again, but my mother does what she's told, and then she starts to cry. We've reached a rainbow in Tombstone, and though it feels overwrought, too on-the-nose, this is what happens. In my dream, each of us begins to cry, because we believe this means what we think it means, which is that no one will die on this trip, in a Quality Inn somewhere off the I-10 in New Mexico. It's not lost on me that in my dream it's the same Quality Inn that I have passed through before—once alone, and once with Bobby when we were also still full of hope, driving as far west as we could get together.

But of course my parents and I have to sleep on this trip. And that is when I'm scared all over again. I lie awake next to my mother while my father is in the other queen bed, next to us, tossing and turning. My mother is wheezing next to me, and I am so used to her labored breathing that when I don't hear it, I reach over and touch her face to make sure she's still alive. I check to make sure her skin is still warm to the touch.

When my father suddenly becomes silent in his own sleep, I get up and touch his face, too. I do this all night—touch their faces to make sure they're still alive. The next morning they laugh when they tell me how they woke up to me stroking their faces in the night.

I don't want to cry in front of them, so I go to the continental breakfast in the lobby to get them coffee. It is filled with aging boomers watching TV and eating waffles from the waffle maker and drinking hot, bad coffee. They don't even look at me, because I am a ghost to them. We are all here at a stopover to somewhere better.

The thing with these kinds of journeys and these kinds of dreams is that the truck stops don't change, the rest stops don't change, the signs telling you that dangerous snakes and scorpions lie just beyond the entrance to a bathroom you've been waiting forty miles to get to don't change, the roads littered with remnants of blown-out tires don't change, the freight trains rattling beside you don't change, the dust devils blowing high and wide in the fallow fields you drive by don't change. The motel bars and empty motel pools don't change. But each time you pass through, you have changed.

In my dream, I think I may have found a way to keep them alive. It's when I wake up that I'm not so sure.

5.

Bethanny had gently manipulated us into performing our pain in our first session. In our second, a week later, she wanted to talk about how the exercise made us feel.

She had asked us to journal about it so we could remember being in the moment, while also journaling after we had some time to process. I'd bought a plain Moleskine for these sessions and had not yet gotten comfortable with doing anything more than a bullet-point list of my anguished embarrassment at performing vulnerability in front of other people. I knew my answers were angry and focused on the humiliation. I had underlined "emotional manipulation" twice. But I had finally started sleeping more than a couple hours a night again, so I decided to come back.

As people raised their hands to share, I looked around and did not see Andrew in the assembled group. I knew he wasn't going to come back, but nobody seemed to be preoccupied by that but me.

As Nathan spoke, offering perfectly healthy pain-avoidance techniques—upping your serotonin, taking trips to the gym, having a good talk with a friend—I watched the room around me crumble. Women talked about their breakthroughs and started weeping again as men wiped the earnest beginnings of tears from their eyes. They had reached higher ground, had gone deeper into their tragedy, but Nathan had been stuck with me and my shitty avoidance techniques: *the inability to feel anything*, which I had been perfecting for over three decades. But I could tell he withheld from me, too. I wasn't sure if he assumed I couldn't take it, or if he hadn't considered how performatively healthy his avoidance techniques were.

"I run" seemed to be loaded, like it could go another way. I run from people. I run from situations. Maybe I wanted him to be more fucked up than he was presenting himself to be.

Bethanny opened up the discussion to talk about how grief impacted people on the molecular level. We talked about how that grief infected our day-to-day lives and made us less efficient people than we wanted to be. I was an efficient person. It's all I had ever wanted to be. The people around me talked about anger over parking spaces, anger over women who had not accepted their love, anger about partners who ignored them over text. These were ways their grief made them act out. We were here trying to transcend pain, which would in turn help everyone articulate the bigger stuff so we could teach ourselves—and eventually our clients—to move on. But some of us (me) could not articulate it, and could not move on.

I wondered how Bobby would answer the questions posed to us. Not that I'd ever want him to join. This was my place to evolve into being a better person. Not his. These grievers were my people, even if I did not fully appreciate them yet. Already there was a certain satisfaction knowing that someone like Debbie, with her short, indistinct bob of mousy brown hair and a penchant for wearing faded floral prints, would be in the front row, to the right, ready to raise a hand when Bethanny asked for someone to share on the topic of "How can we give comfort to the families of the dying?" Immediately I could tell she wanted to be the most engaged person in the training. The most adept at reaching the kind of understanding that would allow her effortlessly to help a person pass into the next realm. It seemed as though Debbie just couldn't help being type A, even about this.

Debbie thought giving comfort was incredibly important, though she had not been given enough during her own family situation. Bethanny's question led Debbie on a journey into how she had just joined a dating app after her grandmother's passing because she was worried that she was never going to have an emergency contact.

"As I scrolled through my phone, I realized there wasn't a single person in there I would put as a beneficiary for my 401(k)," she said. "Do you know how scary that is?"

I stared at her as she looked around the room waiting for an acknowledgment that we all understood the feeling.

"I kept scrolling and realized I wasn't even sure who to call in case of an emergency. Like, what if I fell and cracked my head open and had to go to the hospital—who would I tell? What if I didn't make it? I didn't even fill in anyone for my life-insurance policy. I have money to give no one. It ends with me. That's it."

If I left Bobby I wouldn't have an emergency contact, either. I could put my parents down as beneficiaries, but that felt like a fundamental misunderstanding of how the flow of inheritance was supposed to work. Who would I have after they were gone? I was an only child. The line ended with me, too. I never put Bobby as my beneficiary for anything, as if I was preparing for something in the future that would certainly not be good, but he didn't know that.

I had taken to looking at the money in my 401(k) and

agonizing over whether I should cash it out or not. The sum seemed so small that it would never accrue into anything meaningful anyway, so why couldn't I just take it and start over?

Debbie's voice filled the room, and her dread filled me with dread, too. She said she was on the hunt for someone worthy of being a beneficiary, but not a husband per se (who was she kidding?). We were of varying ages in this room, but it felt like we had all somehow misjudged the big life events. We were focused on the end because we had already fucked up the middle part. We were flailing. Or maybe just I was flailing. People out in the world were filling their social-media feeds with momentous life changes like weddings and babies and new, serious jobs, and though some people in this room might have been doing just that, too, I was not. I had hit a point of stagnation, and I felt like I was dying.

Nathan found me after our session and said it was great to see me again. Self-assessments were intense, he told me. But they would be more intense to perform on our clients. He sensed that I would be a beneficial member in the group. He hugged me for a long time as we were leaving. It felt strange to have a man's body envelop me, a body that did not belong to Bobby. I liked it.

When I got home from the training, I decided to tell Bobby I was going to a workshop to help people grieve.

"A support group," he said.

"No, it's a workshop."

"What are you grieving?"

"It's not for *my* grief."

"I feel like you start something new every week. A beading workshop. Spin class."

"That's vaguely insulting."

"That wasn't my intent, but if you took it that way maybe there's something to it."

I had a choice. Either I could continue down the path of a fight or I could deflect and pivot. I had become a master of avoidance, even when Bobby wanted to go headlong into an argument about what I always perceived as my deficiencies.

"People have a lot of feelings."

"So you're where you belong," he said, a smile growing on his face.

"I don't really have feelings like that," I said.

"There's nothing wrong with having feelings, Evelyn."

"I either have too many or too few for you."

"Sometimes I wonder if you know yourself at all," he said.

I hadn't told him I had lost my job. And that I was going to be an exit guide full-time. I didn't feel like telling him any more after that. Besides, he wasn't a person who liked hearing the details. He was a broad-strokes kind of guy. He made judgments about things pretty quickly, and it was usually that people had a long way to go to be evolved.

He always sort of acted as though he thought he had married a different kind of person.

I said, "Bobby, how do you avoid pain?"

Not as a trap, but because I genuinely wanted to know.

"What kind of question is that after I haven't seen you all day?"

"That was the question we had to ask in group," I said. "Today we talked about our answers."

"What were yours?"

"The normal stuff."

"Self-care or some bullshit?"

"Drugs are the new self-care," I said.

"You answered drugs?"

"It was a joke. I don't really do drugs anymore."

"You smoke."

"Vapors, not smoke. And that's doctor-prescribed. I'm surprised you're so puritanical."

I smiled at him in a breezy way, but he wasn't in the mood for jokes.

"What did you want to get for dinner?" Bobby asked.

This question, though innocuous, had become loaded in the way it does when a person has been in a relationship longer than a year. It is full of feelings of burden and also comes at such a frequency—daily—that it was hard not to mark the passage of time with the question. Thirty-six hundred requests for dinner, give or take, which had morphed into an accusation over the course of our time together.

It also made me feel like I had some fundamental misunderstanding of what it meant to be a wife. A wife was supposed to care about these things. A wife was supposed to want to move forward with her husband into a life filled with children, and a house, and couple vacations where other couples and their children also vacationed.

"I'm not hungry," I said.

"What am I supposed to eat, then?"

I took a deep breath and looked at him and shrugged my shoulders.

He picked up his keys and left the house.

While he was gone, I filled out the paperwork to cash out my 401(k). Twenty-five thousand dollars could float me for a while, so I could finish my training and start working with clients. I wasn't going to spend it frivolously. It was just a cushion.

And then I could get enough money from helping clients that I could just put it back. I also had a credit card with a nineteen-thousand-dollar limit and no balance. Worst-case scenario, I reasoned.

At first, I thought it made me uneasy that we were getting paid to be exit guides, but Bethanny told us it was labor and we were performing a service. Our clients understood this, and no one had ever complained. She didn't tell us what the breakdown was—what she got. But, judging by her general demeanor, I assumed it was fair.

I went to take a shower and thought about Nathan's hands on me.

6.

Bethanny said it was important for us to take a break between our second and third sessions, because that was when things got really intense. She wanted us to spend two weeks feeling our feelings and to write down anything that came up for us around what it might feel like to face death ourselves. But I wasn't afraid of dying. What I was afraid of was having everyone I loved die and being left behind.

When Bethanny called on us to summarize our deepest fears around death during our third session, I said just that.

She nodded and said, "Pain avoidance."

No one seemed to judge me for it, though. They all had their own issues—not having enough time to say goodbye to their loved ones, dying in a horrible accident, suffering unnecessarily. We all nodded at each new vocalized fear, so that everyone could feel supported, and some people even murmured, "Thank you."

When we took a break, I stared at my phone and the lack of text messages from Bobby and killed time listening to everyone else relate to one another. It was easier for me just to stare down at my shoes and fixate on how scuffed they were than to try to find something nice to say about someone else's worst fears. I didn't trust people who were instantly warm.

After Bethanny told us to take our seats, she went from row to row, handing out packets. She said this was the practical-application part of the course, and it would likely take the rest of our six-hour session to get through it.

"This is one of the first things you'll do with the client as they prepare for self-deliverance."

She smiled as she handed out the packets.

"You'd be amazed how many people don't do this for themselves."

The packet reached me, and I pulled out its contents. On top was a health directive to fill out.

"We're going to do it for ourselves now."

There was contact information to fill out and questions about whether you wanted to be buried or cremated and if you wanted a funeral. I hadn't thought of my funeral, but I knew I wanted to be cremated. When I got to the Personal Self-Assessment Chart (PSAC), I held my pen over the empty checklist boxes, wondering how much I valued my life and, more pressingly, what weaknesses I could stand to live with. Bethanny explained that the rationale behind doing the PSAC was that in order to help strangers with their transitions, you had to be prepared for your own.

She assured us that spouses usually couldn't pull the plug, so I didn't feel bad not putting Bobby down as my contact person here, either. Bethanny said it wasn't a shortcoming; they just cared too much. We were to ask someone else we trusted with the paperwork. I would decide that later.

How it worked was, the PSAC started at 100 percent, which

meant you had 100 percent of your faculties. If you were involved in an accident and could walk away with full self-care, normal intake of food and drink, and full consciousness, then you were still at full capacity. But, really, the macabre joke was, who could say any of us were ever operating at 100 percent? From there, faculties decreased in 10-percent increments, starting with "some evidence of disease" at 90 percent. By 80 percent, although someone could still fully care for herself and maintain the same level of activity, suddenly work came with *some* effort. Nutrient intake was just beginning to be reduced, though the bright spot was lucidity and full consciousness. By 60 percent, mobility was reduced and disease was significant; consciousness could waver between full, drowsy, and confused.

It went on and on like this, down to a 0-percent PSAC, which was, of course, dead. We were to choose our personal preferences to correspond with each assessment: DNR, IV, feeding tube, or "extra help"—i.e., blood transfusions, dialysis, transplants.

Did I want someone to care for me? Did it matter that at 50 percent I mainly had to lie down or at the very least sit still? At what point would I request a final exit? I thought about how selfish, at each increment, it would be to stay alive. How much I was willing to put out those around me. Whether or not I wanted artificial nutrition or an IV was not something I had previously considered. Did I want a blood transfusion or dialysis? I don't know—both? I was healthy, active, and only thirty-seven. Despite my morbid fascinations, I hadn't exactly envisioned myself in a hospital bed surrounded by pacing loved ones, with cords, tubes, and other things coming off my person.

I looked around the room at the others furiously scribbling their final wishes and chastised myself for being so ill-prepared to consider what an acceptable, if suboptimal, life meant for me. Debbie seemed to be finished already, rushing her errorless quiz to the front. Bethanny waved her hand and whispered to Debbie to go back to her seat, which she sheepishly did. Debbie, Debbie, Debbie. You were certainly the kind of person who needed to be the best, or, at the very least, the first in everything you did. It was admirable. In some ways, we were all striving in these rooms. We weren't people trying to avoid the inevitable. But what bothered me is that I fixated on Debbie. Somewhere along the way—with my third therapist, perhaps—it occurred to me that the flaws you see in someone else are the flaws you need to work on yourself. But I wasn't anything like Debbie.

I tried to peek at the directives of the people sitting in my row. To my left was a perky blonde who looked to have settled nicely into her fifties. I remembered her name was Monica. She wanted out at 30 percent—totally bedbound. I stared at the side of her Botoxed face, her expensive highlights. She had the confidence of someone who knew she would be on the receiving end of excellent care. I suspected someone at home truly loved her. Either she feared death and wanted to wait until near the bitter end to go, or she knew something I didn't. Perhaps she just had a robust relationship with God.

To my right was Ponytail Richard. Richard was balding on top and had the remnants of a long curly mane in a slicked-down ponytail. With a dozen empty seats available, Richard had chosen to sit next to me, not even a seat between us. It was too close. Richard wanted to go at 20 percent. I scanned the chart. Under intake, "minimal sips" was listed; he'd be fully reliant on an IV, and yet Richard still felt life would be worth living. Why?

I felt insane. Fifty percent, maybe even 60 percent, is where

I landed. But if I was telling the truth, it was really somewhere more like 70 percent. I had never had a strong will to live.

Did I simply not want to be a burden? Or did I believe no one would want the burden of me?

I leaned over to Richard and touched his paper.

"You missed a column," I said.

"What?" he asked, startled.

"Uh, you didn't check off 'feeding tube,'" I said.

"I don't want one," he said.

"But how will you make it to twenty percent without a feeding tube?"

"There are ways," he said, and looked at me as if I didn't know anything at all.

"Okay, that's fine."

"Do you know you're more likely to die from an infection due to them jamming that fucking thing down your throat?"

"No."

"Yeah, that's how they got my mother. I'm not going down that way."

I told him I was sorry for his loss.

"She didn't have to, that's my point."

I told him I was sorry again.

"Have you ever even seen a feeding tube being inserted?"

"No," I said.

"Google it."

He nodded at me like he wanted me to do it right there. Under so much pressure, I took out my phone and did. WebMD had a whole page about what it was like to have a feeding tube inserted. It was disturbing. He told me to google YouTube videos that illustrated the insertion techniques. I whispered that I would watch them later.

"What did he say?" Monica asked.

"My mother," Richard said, before dropping off into silence. Perhaps he decided it wasn't worth it.

Monica looked at me, expectant.

"He has an issue with feeding tubes."

I said it as if Richard wasn't listening to me minimize his catastrophe.

"My issue is with infection," he said.

"I'm sorry," I said again.

Back on my chart, I saw my checkmark next to "feeding tube" and felt like an idiot. No one had told me they were bad. How could we make life decisions here without all the facts?

I raised my hand.

"Excuse me," I said.

Bethanny looked up. "Yes?" she asked, lowering her glasses.

"What's your opinion on feeding tubes?"

"They're a personal preference, really."

"But what about infection?" I asked.

"That's always a possibility."

Richard must have felt vindicated in some way. I shot glances at the others. They looked as if I'd somehow fucked up their decision-making process the same way Richard had done to mine. This was real, but in many ways it still felt like a game: we weren't anticipating death for ourselves quite yet.

"What do you mean, infection?" a woman in the front row asked.

"It's a violent operation," Richard said.

"Have you ever seen a feeding tube inserted? It's ghastly," Bethanny said.

The word "ghastly" sounded luxurious when she said it.

Everyone looked down at their directives, suddenly concerned.

"But it really is a personal preference."

She slid her glasses back up the bridge of her nose and went back to reading whatever she was reading.

I wanted to know what Nathan's threshold was before I wanted to know anything else about him. Nathan was the only other person I'd met here who did not break into spontaneous tears. He wasn't a notetaker, either; instead, he just nodded his head in infinite understanding. As if he'd remember it all, no problem. I knew there was something going on under the surface. That he was seeking something, too.

Bethanny looked up and asked if we were ready. There were murmurs in the group. One person broke the tension by saying, "I'm pretty sure my family's not going to like this."

We all laughed.

I settled on 50 percent. Final answer. I didn't want to be bedridden or to need assistance, but I also didn't want to seem like a person who gave up so easily. Simply thinking about relinquishing that kind of control gave me anxiety.

It was true that I had become an observer in my life, of my life. *Go with it* was a mantra. *Going with it* meant I never had to be held accountable for anything because nothing was ever my choice—or, at the very least, not my idea. But making this my new life path was my idea.

Though here, too, we were still just observers. Some in the group confided in us that they had been nurses frustrated by how long you had to wring out the last drops of life, whether the patient liked it or not. We wanted to learn another way to be helpers.

One woman's father had committed suicide, and then her

boyfriend did, too. Finally, her mother had traveled to Switzerland to end her life with Dignitas, the group at the forefront of the death-with-dignity movement. Her mother was not terminal, the woman said. She was chronically depressed, though to me that felt like a terminal illness. The woman didn't find out her mother's plans until after her mother was dead—and learned it from a letter she received postmarked Airmail. In it, her mother apologized, but said she saw no alternative. And she hoped her daughter could understand. How could someone quantify the daughter's grief? What were the people left behind supposed to do with the knowledge that their need wasn't enough to stick around for? Bethanny told us to focus on the client, but all that collateral damage needed a place to go, too.

Bethanny said people struggle with the idea that some big final revelation will come as they prepare for the end, that the dying will finally make sense of the suffering faced in their lives. But who can say if that moment will ever come? Often, it's just small understandings that come too late—after a parent is already dead and gone, or an ex-wife has moved on. That's what the letters were for: the people who survived the dead.

"Those of you who have been in recovery—and you don't have to self-identify—know that making amends is very powerful. It gives you relief," Bethanny said. "Making amends before you die allows you to exit peacefully."

She walked around us and put her hand on Nathan's shoulder.

"There is no greater gift we can give a person than helping them make amends before they pass. It is our job to help them feel safe enough to write down their thoughts and feelings toward those who they may have wronged and let go of their guilt and shame."

Bethanny faced us and smiled. "That they entrust us with taking the letters of amends and let us send them to their loved ones . . . that's powerful," she said. "And it's a chance to give their souls freedom."

It felt powerful to know I could be privy to someone's worst actions. But the thought also filled me with guilt and shame. I didn't want to hold anything over anyone—especially not our clients.

But it was hard not to admit there was something remarkable about being able to have this kind of access to where someone was most tender.

7.

When I got home, the apartment was empty, and I didn't even turn on any lights as I made my way to the bedroom. But I was worried about what kind of dreams I would have.

A year before I started working with Bethanny, my father had just finished recuperating from his first hospital stay when I suggested we take a family trip to the desert. I flew into El Paso and we took off from there. Though I didn't want the trip to feel like it could be our last, it took on the tone of being crucial anyway. Residue from that trip had plagued my dreams since.

My father's dreams had been fighting dreams for as long as he could remember. I could relate, because my dreams had so often been consumed with terror that I frequently moaned and wept in my sleep. Bobby didn't know what was happening the first time. He just shook me awake, terrified. In my father's dreams he was always fighting people who had wronged him.

He never wanted to lose. He once told us about the three boys who had jumped him, how he'd hunted each one of them down afterward and fought them fairly—one-on-one. Even in the third grade my father was tough. He put the last boy in the hospital, beating him within an inch of his life with bottles and whatever else he could find in the street. This was not out of the ordinary for the time and place he grew up in. His own father beat him for it, but not with his usual severity: he was proud of his son for fighting back. When my father told me, so was I. This is who we are, I thought. This is how we survive. I wanted my father to want to survive. I believed he still did, even if it didn't seem like it from the outside. I took up the job of his survival with fervor. I wanted him to see how alike we were, and if I could try to survive, then he could, too.

THE FIRST NIGHT of our trip together, we rented a hotel room in a roadside efficiency hotel—not the kind you make a reservation for, but the kind you hope still has rooms by the time you're too tired to keep driving.

In the darkness of the hotel room, my father fought a bear in his sleep and kicked over the coffee table next to the sofa he was sleeping on. I had learned to be on high alert—variations of breathing patterns, sounds of distress—from years of listening through doorways. My mother and I were sharing the bed, and we heard a loud crash. She shook my shoulder, thinking I was asleep. "I know," I whispered. We were worried that he was dying, and that he had to go to the hospital again. She jumped out of bed and made it across the room to shake him awake even before I had a chance to move. I crawled out of bed to pour water from the bathroom sink into a glass for him. He sipped it as my mother touched his face with a kind of tenderness I had never seen from her before. It must have been the person she turned into during these late-night scenarios, during the kind of moments I had never been privy to.

He told us that in his dream he was on the street, and he heard freight trains first, then the bear. He said he fought it to protect me, and for a moment I thought I saw my mother look jealous. She had been with him every night through all of this and she wanted all of him in return.

That was the first time I watched him fight someone in his dreams. It seemed like a new development, but my mother later told me he had been fighting all along. At first, I thought he was choking. Throwing up like you do when your pancreas is failing you. But he was just trying to protect me.

We were in one of the darkest parts of the country, no light pollution reaching across the desert to us, save the few lights that dotted the parking lot full of cars with license plates from different parts of the country, and whatever light bounced off the highway nearby. We could see the Milky Way.

Earlier in the evening I had watched from the front door as my father slowly walked across the parking lot to the convenience store to see if he could buy beer. My mother was still in the habit of begging him not to, but I never tried to stop him, because I always wanted some for myself. He would buy me whatever he was drinking so he would not have to drink by himself. Sitting with him meant talking to him and trying to make him feel less alone. Like he wasn't doing anything bad—he was normal, and I was normal. We had to hide our hangovers from her. It was an unspoken pact we shared while my mother looked on and counted how many cans we opened between the two of us. She must have counted tens of thousands of cans being opened in her lifetime. What a hobby to have!

Under the Milky Way I watched as my father walked back across the parking lot with a six-pack of Shiner Bock and a brown paper bag. The bag held bottles of cider for me, and he pulled them out while my mom frowned at us both. We were a team, and each complicit in what was happening to the other.

On the trip I could tell he was having trouble remembering things, or was confused by things that seemed simple to us. It made him angry, scared. If I had to guess, at that time my father was 80 percent on the PSAC: some evidence of disease; normal activity and work "with some effort."

In the morning, as always, we pretended nothing happened. We wanted to believe it, really. We woke up as if we didn't hear him whimper. As if we weren't afraid he'd collapse each time he got up to go to the bathroom.

On the second night of our trip, I found myself trailing after my father in the streets of a dark desert town, peering into lit-up gas stations, hoping they would have whatever we wanted and we wouldn't have to walk anymore.

He had downed three bourbons in the hotel bar before he took off into the streets to find cheap beer. I was only on my second drink when my mother hissed at me that I was no better than him and went upstairs by herself. I didn't want him outside alone, getting hurt or into trouble. I finished my drink quickly and paid the bill and ran into the street, looking for him. He hadn't made it far: he was standing on a nearby street corner, looking around, confused. He did not see me, but, looking at him from afar, I began to worry. I could sense the urgency of his need as he looked from his phone to the street and to his phone again.

We were seemingly the only people wandering the streets of this tiny town, and his anxiety level was high. I had noticed a border patrol truck passing us more than once during our beer walk.

"I'm cold," I said. "My stomach hurts."

I don't know why I was reverting back to childhood excuses as reasons we should turn back. They didn't work, because he didn't care, and so we pressed on. While he peered into windows, I watched a freight train pass through the middle of town, cutting the quiet night with a deep rumbling and blaring horn. I wanted to follow it out of town, toward the still-bright horizon, back to Los Angeles.

WE WERE ON an endless journey for more alcohol, and all I could think of was that if we had just brought some in the car with us I wouldn't be standing in the cold, peering into a shut-down gas station, arguing about whether we should knock.

"They'll appreciate the business," he said.

"There's no one in there."

"I think I see someone in the back."

"It doesn't look like it's been opened for years. Can we go back to the hotel?" I asked.

And it went back and forth like this as we walked, until, finally, he gave up. I stared at the sky above us and saw more clusters of stars than I had ever seen before. I wondered if the people who lived here took it for granted. Back in the room, my mother asked where we had gone, as if she didn't know already. It was a game we always played while on vacation. Where did Dad go? As if he didn't always go on the same hunt.

I stayed awake and listened to the ghostly horn of the freight trains passing through town, warning people off the tracks, and thought about how this area was known to be spiritual. The nearby Chisos Mountains meant *Ghost Mountains*, and sometimes they were said to cast an eerie glow. Folklore said the devil lived in the caves and in the mountains. But the recent inhabitants had no idea what skittered across this land, whether ghost or devil.

Other people said that this land was primed for odd things to happen, for miracles. The belief was so strong that each night people clustered at a viewing station nearby and waited for alien lights to glow. They didn't realize that what they saw was just car headlights weaving back and forth across the horizon from a border town sixty miles away. There had been decades of stories about people who sought religion in the hills around this desert. There were even churches built into mountains, and people said the sculptures of Christ sweated real moisture into the land. But mostly people just came here to get lost after their lives fell apart. It was a place where you could still get away with pretending to be someone else.

The next morning we drove past ghost towns in the desert, wooden posts made into crosses cascading over the sides of the hills surrounding them. I pulled the car to the side of the road, and we walked through a cemetery, past homemade headstones and rocks placed on top of dirt so animals wouldn't dig up the remains of people who had lived and died here. I remembered a story I had read about one of these people in a local paper, the people who came to the desert to live their own way in adobe houses on unpaved roads called Easy Street and Utopia Road. The story was full of superstition, as stories about the desert always were. It went like this:

Martin Spangler's property was surrounded by hundreds of acres of sagebrush-covered hills. He knew the devil was out there, in the caves and on the hilltops, just watching him. It was no secret that spirits haunted this land. He had seen the unexplainable in the sky and on the land more than once. It was part of living out here. It was just something else to get used to, along with loneliness and a need for self-reliance.

Martin used to have horses, a burro, and two wolflike mutts, but they knew what was happening and had since run away. The dogs he pushed away, because they were very loyal creatures. The horses ran and he did not have the strength to give chase. Instead, he sat down in a lawn chair in front of his trailer and thought about what to do.

He decided he would dig.

In the early evening, when the sun was barreling toward its finish and the heat was loosening, he found his shovel in the makeshift shed, and looked out around the property. Five acres had seemed like a lot once, but it really wasn't. Not that anyone had tucked in near his sagebrush-and-sand-covered property out in the desert. No one else had come out this far to settle a patch in order to fall off the face of the earth, just him.

He didn't want to be too near the house, because he didn't want the cesspool he had built underneath to taint his final resting place. He found a faraway spot by the rocks he had put down to prevent his land from washing away during mid-spring rainstorms. The rocks would be his barricade from washing down the road, or floating up. He would have to tell someone to make sure to weigh the spot down with some good, thick quartz rock, and maybe mark it with a nice piece of jasper. He began to dig. He knew digging a grave would be a multi-day affair and so he took his time. He was not at all operating at his best anyway.

Yesterday he was involved in the business of the world, but soon he would not be. It was okay as far as Martin was concerned. He had been waiting for the end and was not at all afraid. His cells would leave his body with his spirit and all that energy would be dispersed into the sky and the clouds. His mother was up there and his father, too. His sweet daughter was another mass of energy that hovered above his trailer day in and day out. He could feel her there, waiting for him so he could tease her mercilessly once again.

Dig and dig he did.

When he was finished, dusk had just settled into that soft blue light that he liked so much. He watched the vibrant pinks and purples fill the sky and the stubborn light refuse to leave the horizon, spreading out in a line. Sometimes, Martin said, he felt like he was a tumbleweed stopped against a fence at the end of the earth. He saw tumbleweeds plow through his land from time to time with bits and scraps from people's lives—clothes and junk, mostly. But it still made him wonder how people and things traveled over the land, unbridled, stopped only by force or fence.

When he was finished digging his own grave a few days later, Martin called his friends. He still had a few, and he asked them to stop by for a party if they felt like it. They came to pay their respects. They did not try to convince him to go to doctors or the hospital or anything like that. They knew he wanted to die under the stars and he did just that.

He had asked someone to stop by in a couple of days, just to check on him, and when his friend came upon the trailer, he saw that Martin was dead but his dogs were back, watching over the body so no animals would get to him. They were loyal, after all.

His story was printed in a flimsy paper my mother and I had picked up as we came through this area when she took me out of L.A. before, to help save me. She read it out loud as we drove through the desert, and it stuck with us both.

"Remember the man who dug his own grave?" she'd ask me sometimes.

"Martin Spangler," I'd say.

We both stared at the picture they'd printed of him. He looked content, free. His was a conscious death.

I thought about Martin as I came back to the car, my parents already inside, both afraid of cemeteries, of dwelling on death, and we pressed on.

"Remember the guy who dug his own grave?" I asked.

"I was just thinking about him," my mother said.

"What?" my father asked from the back seat.

"He died," she said.

"Why do you talk about this stuff?" he asked.

"She's obsessed," my mother said, pointing at me.

In Van Horn, we caught the I-10 west and headed into New Mexico, then continued north along two-lane highways that brought us through forgotten towns with crumbling asphalt roads, between vast green hills dotted with cattle. We were on a mission to find a church where pilgrims came from all over the world to collect sacred dirt from a hole in the ground. When we drove up to the adobe church, I could already make out crutches hanging from a fence that wound up the walkway. We all got out of the car and went in separate directions, my mother focused on finding her way inside the church as my father meandered through the grass to a stone altar covered in silk flowers, prayer candles, and plastic rosary beads.

I walked through an outbuilding with walls covered in hundreds of laminated portraits of people surrounding statues of the Virgin Mary, Our Lady of Guadalupe, Our Lady of La

Vang, and St. Francis. This was the place to bring—and leave—your suffering.

I looked at all the people staring back at me—photos both aged and new, faces both smiling and not—and wondered if they had been cured. As I walked on, I saw more crutches and braces and medallions embossed with saints. St. Jude seemed to be the most popular. There were a few people praying in the outbuilding, and I walked out, not wanting to disturb. My father had disappeared, and I wandered into the church. It was a simple room with a dirt-covered floor and stained-glass windows showing the Stations of the Cross. I stared at Jesus, bleeding and carrying his own cross. My mother was on a kneeler, praying, as a priest started a mass devoted to a couple whose names he struggled to pronounce. The adobe church was filled with lit devotional candles that had pictures of St. Jude printed on them. We were all coming here with our hopeless cases.

I ducked into a small room that held the hole in the ground full of dirt. I watched as an older woman who was somewhere in her seventies and missing a canine tooth crouched down low and spooned dirt into a plastic grocery bag. She crossed herself. I smiled at her as she ducked under a low eave and walked back out into the light.

"The gift shop is selling containers," my father whispered behind me. He stood in the curved doorway and handed me a few circular plastic containers.

"Your mother will want one for each of us."

I crouched down and touched the dirt. The hole in the ground couldn't have been more than two feet around. The dirt was fine and soft and cool to the touch. It felt strange, not like the pebbled dirt outside.

"Do you think it's real?" I whispered.

"Why wouldn't it be?"

"I don't know," I said.

"They say you can rub it on the parts of your body that are sick and it'll help," he said, reading a brochure.

I held the dirt in my hand and let it sift through my fingers back into the hole.

"Where are you going to put it?" I asked.

"I should just crawl in there," my father said.

"I thought about that, but it's too small."

He looked back at the brochure while I spooned dirt into a container.

"It says people try to eat it, sprinkle it on their food like salt, but you're not supposed to."

"Why would anyone do that?" I asked.

"I'm sure they think it'll heal them quicker," he said. "People love shortcuts."

"Do you think Mom will try to eat it?"

"That's not funny," he said, but I could tell he was laughing a little bit.

My mother came in and stared at the hole and said, "This is it?"

My father helped her crouch down and she immediately cupped the dirt, pulled her shirt down, and rubbed it on her chest.

"They said don't eat it," I said.

"I won't."

She eyed the hole like she was thinking about it, though.

"I want a candle. Did you get me a candle?"

"I didn't know if you wanted St. Jude or someone else. We can go choose one," my father said. "Will you fill these for your mother?"

"Make sure to fill them up all the way," she said.

I leaned back down over the hole and watched them walk into the light. I stared at the hole and wondered how it could still be so full after people had taken so much from it. I dipped the spoon back in the dirt. But instead of pouring it into the container, I put the spoon in my mouth.

The dirt was dry and tasted like iron, and I was having trouble choking it down. I started coughing and dirt flew out. I covered my mouth as the woman with the plastic grocery bag came back in and stood over me. We stared at each other. She knew what I was trying to do.

Months after the trip, my mother started saying she was going to leave my father. All I could think was: *Where are you going to go?* It felt like a betrayal for her to leave him now. How would she survive? How would he? I knew what it felt like to want to save yourself—to feel like someone else's decline was directly tied to your own—but, still, I didn't want her to leave. It felt like a pre-emptive move—a distancing from the pain that was coming. A kind of pre-grief she wanted to give herself before the actual bad thing, which was most certainly coming as my father continued to drink more heavily. In casual conversation he would say, "I'm trying to die quickly," or "I want to be dead, but it's taking longer than I thought."

My mother and I would roll our eyes.

I had grown up with his desire to die on view. He did not try to hide it even from me, his child. He would say things like "I'd planned on being dead by forty, but it didn't work out that way." My mother had been pre-grieving for the entirety of their marriage. And I joined her when I was born.

8.

I decided to take a seat in the back row when I came to our next training session.

When Bethanny breezed in, she told us we were nearing the end of our self-assessment training and soon we'd be trainees in the field, each of us paired with a seasoned partner.

She gave us tips that we wrote down, including making sure to enter a room silently and not say anything for a few minutes. She said this was so we could pick up the energy of the room, the tenor of a person's suffering. Each person was at a different level of pain and acceptance.

"Hold the room," she said. "People push you away as they're dying. Let their feelings have space so you can gauge your approach in how you'll help them through it. Death isn't something that happens to you, it's something you do."

Bethanny kept driving home that we were active participants in how we chose to die, and I couldn't help but think about how we chose to be active participants in the way we were living, too—or not. Sometimes it felt nearly impossible to step out of that inertia once you were in it.

Bethanny told us she was here to shake us out of the comfortable way we were living, and so she had one more request.

"This is going to be uncomfortable," she said. "But it's important to sit in your uncomfortable feelings."

Bethanny asked us to make a list of the ten physical objects we cared about most in the world. She did not direct us on how to choose. Instead, she talked about inheritance. She said, "Not everything that matters to you will matter to the people you leave behind."

Some people did not want to hear that, but she went on.

"Don't you realize the things that are the most important to you might not matter to the people you love? In fact, those inheritances could be a burden to them."

People around me started murmuring.

"That's a kick in the pants," Richard whispered.

She wanted us to write down what we valued the most.

I stared at a piece of paper numbered one to ten, unable to think of one thing that mattered to me.

I wrote down: "computer."

I felt bad about myself for it. My computer would be obsolete in a few years. The hard drive had pictures of Bobby and me from vacations, from our first apartment together, our first Christmas, and pictures of him sleeping, because I loved the way he looked like a little boy, innocent, like he'd never hurt anyone in his entire life. There were pictures of us with sunburns, on the beach, half a dozen photos with slight variations between them as we tried to get the shot of us just right. Others of sunsets, of mountains—always empty of people—and vastness. Who would I bequeath these to? Digital files in the thousands, an accumulation of our lives that only we wanted to see or maybe neither of us wanted to see anymore. There were pictures of my life before him. It was all separated by year, tidily organized for optimal viewing.

Numbers two to ten. I cared about things, inanimate objects, small items from flea markets that I had found, or, better yet, that we had found together. But were they the most important things to me? No.

Bethanny said, "Don't write 'computer.'"

I looked up and heard grumbling around me.

"Don't tell me you wrote down 'computer,'" she said to all of us. A few people looked around to see who had done it—who had so little going for them. I saw others cross out a line on their paper; I wasn't the only one. But did Debbie write down "computer," too? Did Monica? Did Nathan?

"A computer is your most precious object?"

She was scolding us, as if she was better than us. The woman next to me fingered the gold necklaces she was wearing, and I knew they were going on her list. She saw me staring at them and said, "I'm giving them to my daughters."

One necklace for each daughter. How would she choose?

I had still not added anything else to my list. "Wedding ring" wasn't the first thing I wrote down, even though it was the best thing I owned. People I didn't know liked to admire it and give me compliments on it. Bobby had it made custom. He thought about the things I liked and put them into a ring design—a band of diamond chips with our names inscribed on the side, where only I could see the detail. When he gave it to me, I thought, *I will love this man forever.* Maybe I knew I wanted to be buried with it, no matter what. I wanted it to be an achievement no one could ever take away from me, even in death. *I did this*, even if I did it poorly.

I added a piece of art that I loved—a drawing of a dead owl a friend had given me as a gift. It was representative of a spirit leaving a body, and I hung it over my side of the bed so I could look at it every morning.

Bobby said, "That's grim." But I didn't think so.

I also wrote down: "framed photograph of a night swimming pool."

The pool was empty and full of possibility, and from time to time I'd look at it before bed, hoping it would end up in my dreams. Sometimes that worked.

I crossed out "computer" and left my list at three. Bethanny told us time would be up soon. I wondered what she had put on her list. She was a very spiritual person, which I found admirable. Not the kind of spiritual that lined her pockets with crystals and weighed down her neck with amulets. She was low-key about her spirituality in a way that felt attainable for those of us who were struggling to find peace. She had collected us through her website's information form and e-mails from curious people, asking what it meant to help someone die. Then she vetted us carefully. Just like how she collected our clients. She told us about her own mother's death, which was a way to say she was just like us—a person who knew deep loss. Her mother was private, she said. Bethanny didn't know she was sick until her mother left her a letter saying she was going off to die. Bethanny had no closure with her mother. That's why she had made having closure her mission—for both the dying and those left behind. Sometimes I thought Bethanny got off on maybe being a guru or something.

It was strange to die in private, hidden away like that. It made me think of animals that wandered away to die in peace and alleviated any kind of burden of grief. I thought about watching my dog die. We had waited too long, hoping he would go naturally. Instead, he had taken to hobbling into the garden with his arthritic limbs and lying down in the bushes to wait. But he wasn't dying. He was suffering. I had told my parents I would take him to be euthanized, because I knew they couldn't. I couldn't, either, but it felt like what a strong person was supposed to do. And I was nothing if not perpetually strong, even at twenty-five. I had made it my mission in life to be strong—*to be unflappable.* So there I was, considering how easily he had jumped into our family car, wondering if maybe it was too soon after all. As we stared at each other in the rearview mirror, I began to wonder if he knew what was happening and if he felt I was his betrayer.

In the clinic, I led him into a small room with a stainless-steel table. I was worrying about how I would get him on the table, but he kept walking toward the door, wanting to leave. I could only think that he was trying to tell me it wasn't time yet. I petted him, feeling the outline of his bones, marveling at how much body mass he had lost in just the last few years. The vet gave us time together, but more time felt excruciating. Even as I tried to comfort him, I couldn't help but feel I was complicit in his death, just as I had been complicit in his prolonged suffering. And here, now, I hoped that he knew how much I would miss him. I sobbed while the doctor hovered over my dog, who sat on his haunches on a blanket on the floor as the doctor looked for a vein in his paw.

I kept a hand on him so he knew he wasn't alone. And then, as the medication took hold, he deflated, folding in on himself. It was as if his spirit escaped him and all that was left was the shell of a body. He slid down to lie on the floor, and the veterinarian gently helped him. His prolonged suffering was what stuck with me most. To me, that was the cruelty of a prolonged death. Bethanny told us to put down our pencils.

"You'll wrap one of these items up and bring it back here for our next session," she said, "and give it to someone in this room."

People were beside themselves as she stood in front of us and smiled.

"It's okay, I know you can do it."

When I came home, I looked around the apartment to see what I would be willing to part with. It wasn't that I had attachment issues to anything; it was more like I didn't feel attached to anything at all. I looked at all the things that it wouldn't hurt me to leave and understood that being too detached might actually be my problem.

9.

When we gathered again, people had their items covered in Christmas holly or balloons or other festive wrapping they'd found in their houses. We all looked around nervously as Bethanny went to the front of the room. I wondered if others thought this was a stunt, or if they would have to part with the things they loved most. I looked down at the little velvet box I was holding and prepared myself to leave if it wasn't.

"How do you feel right now?" Bethanny asked, smiling.

We laughed nervously and peered around at each other.

Richard raised his hand. "I waited until the last minute to choose. It wasn't until last night that I laid everything out."

"And what happened?"

"I started crying, because I didn't want to give anything away."

"That's your suffering."

Richard looked at her, open-faced and humble. "I know," he said.

"Did you even know how attached you were to your objects? Did it surprise you?"

"I've carried them around with me through moves, through everything, for years," Richard said. "Sometimes I think they're all I have."

"But in your last days, these objects will be completely meaningless. And if you're ruled by these objects, you aren't really free."

We nodded. We were the children of late capitalism.

"Do you want to be surrounded by all the objects you love when you're dying? Do you think that's a good idea?"

She walked up and down the aisles around us. No one answered. We were waiting for her to tell us what to do.

"No," she said. "It's not."

"To see everything you're leaving behind will only fill you with the gravity of your loss."

I looked down at my velvet box and turned it around and around in my palm. I hadn't even bothered to wrap it. I stared at my naked ring finger and the white outline my ring had left.

"Our attachments are what cause our suffering. To detach with love is to free yourself from this suffering. This is what we're helping our clients through. But we have to step through it first."

Heads around me nodded. People took notes.

"Around the deathbed we must instead put pictures of people who have already passed rather than pictures of people they will be leaving behind," Bethanny said. "You don't want them to be in distress because of what they're leaving behind. We do not want to prolong their suffering. We want them to leave full of gratitude. What we're doing is helping them die without resentments and regrets. I've said it before—it's a profound freedom."

We all clapped. Maybe some of us from the relief that we could carry whatever we had carefully wrapped back home with us.

Bethanny focused on talking about what it would be like to be paired up in the field at the end of our final session. She had talked about bonding, vulnerability, and trust. We were going to build deep relationships with one another.

"It's inevitable," she said.

She had started circling us, and I knew she was about to deliver one of her truth bombs.

"One thing I want to mention that's crucial to this work: we are here in service of our clients. We are of course human beings, but part of relieving them of their suffering is also not giving them our own. Do not make their deaths about yourself," she said.

She looked around the room and seemingly tried to make eye contact with each one of us to make sure we got the point.

"This is difficult work and it's an intimate experience. Be a human."

She looked right at me and said, "I don't expect you to be stone-faced, but please don't burden our clients with your feelings. That's what I and other more seasoned members of the group are here for. Offload with us, not them."

She then told us who we would be paired with for our first client. She said that after watching us she had a good idea of who would be a good pairing and so she made the choice for us. I looked around at who was left from the first session. Ponytail Richard was. Debbie was still with us, of course, and I imagined she had never quit anything in her entire life. Monica had disappeared. Nathan was there, and several people I did not recognize were sitting around him and smiling at the rest of us.

"This is not easy work," Bethanny said. "And while I don't fault those who didn't stick it out, I'm proud of those of you who stayed."

She began to read pairs of names off a roster, and I was

annoyed when I heard her call Debbie and Nathan's names together.

"Evelyn and Lorraine," she said.

Lorraine stood up and looked around the room. I hesitated, but when I finally got up she smiled at me. We paired off and she went in for a hug.

Lorraine was in her sixties, and she usually dressed like she was on her way to yoga and wore a number of beaded bracelets she must have picked up at meditation retreats. I had seen her at the edges of our room before. When she came to our first meeting and introduced herself to us, she had her brown hair in a braided crown. She spent the majority of the meeting slowly unbraiding it and flipping her crinkled locks at the row of people behind her.

10.

Bethanny wanted us to bond outside the confines of the room, so Lorraine wrapped her arm around my shoulders and suggested we go for coffee. She led me to a little sporty Audi, and I wondered how rich she was and how much she was getting paid. She told me she'd gotten into this line of work because she had watched her husband die slowly from ALS. He had been an insurance salesman in Connecticut, where there were few options for how and when to die, so she sat by his side while he deteriorated, and did the best she could.

"I held on too long," Lorraine told me as we idled in the drive-thru, waiting to order coffee. She wanted McDonald's coffee (her favorite), but when she saw the face I made, she decided she'd go to Starbucks instead.

"The line's too long anyway," she said. "People really love McDonald's coffee. Not because it's cheap."

She was trying to put me in my place, I decided.

"It got to the point where he couldn't talk and he was just lying in the hospital bed. But I still wouldn't let them take out the feeding tube."

"That's hard," I said.

"He didn't want to be that way. *I* wanted him that way. I wanted him to stay with me longer. In any capacity."

"I understand."

"I kept asking him: Tell me if you're in pain. Blink if you're in pain. If you're in pain I'll tell them to take the tube away."

She pulled up to the menu.

"What do you want?"

"Venti decaf Americano," I said.

"That's not even a coffee."

I hesitated before saying, "It is."

She shrugged and ordered it anyway.

"He was in pain. He was whimpering. But I couldn't detach. I read all the self-help books about detachment, and then, when it happened, I couldn't detach. I let him suffer. Do you even know what that feels like?"

I knew she wasn't looking for an answer from me, so I handed her money and she looked at it like it didn't make any sense.

"I don't want it."

"Are you sure?"

She waved me away with her hand and inched toward the window.

"They take so long here."

"I'm sorry."

"Bethanny taught me detachment," she said. She looked at me, not with benevolence, but with something else.

"You can't learn this through books. There are hundreds of books on detachment. Go look for yourself! I'm sure you have. But you can't really feel it until you have to experience it yourself. Then you can help people find their way through it. People think there's something noble in suffering. Let me tell you, *there is not.*"

Lorraine pulled into a parking space so she could sip without distraction.

We offered clients two methods: plastic hoods with helium tanks or Seconal cocktails. She told me it was our client's choice and she had worked with both but preferred the cocktail.

"It just feels less gruesome," she said. "Sometimes they reach to take off the hood and you have to hold their arms down."

"Because they changed their mind?"

The idea of a mistake made me nervous.

"They signed a waiver," she said. "We tell them their initial reaction will be to take off the hood. We ask if they want us to stop them from pulling it off, and they say they want to be stopped. They provide us with written confirmation."

She was silent for a minute, staring off into space.

"It's hard to watch that reflex toward self-preservation," she said.

She saw my face and said, "Bethanny administers those. You don't have to."

"Okay," I said, grateful.

We had gone over all of this in the room as a possibility, but Lorraine said she always tried to talk clients out of a hood by giving them the details.

After my first training session, I read online message boards full of comments saying that what we were doing was not providing a conscious way to die. Commenters said you'd actually have to break down each of those Seconal tablets to truly understand what you were undertaking. Different religions had mixed messages about whether or not it was morally wrong. Putting on a hood and twisting a knob, or sipping a cup to make you go to sleep was the ultimate act of control. In some ways, it was an act of defiance. *I will say when I'm ready to go, not you, God.*

Lorraine reiterated how I was to behave with a family, how close to get to the client. We had binders full of questions for each client to answer, in order to help prepare them for their deaths. Not just "Who would you like to have listed in your death directive, to handle your remains, to make the arrangements?" but questions like:

What is the thing that you must forgive yourself for?

and

What day of your life would you like to live over again?

and

Why?

And we were supposed to ask, "How do you define God?"

We were supposed to wait for an answer that felt sufficient. We'd wait as they stumbled through their approximation of what they believed would happen to them once they died. If they felt safe with us. If they were sure.

Lorraine told me she had just come off a difficult case. An aborted attempt. She said the client had chosen the hood. Bethanny worked with a woman who made them, fitted with a terry-cloth closure for comfort, and she ordered them from her custom-made with each new request.

"He was depressed," Lorraine said. "We carefully vet our clients. There is so much paperwork—more than any doctor. The liability, you understand. We don't just send out some simple questionnaire. We look at medical records. They write us a letter about their situation. Bethanny meets with them. I know she went through all of this with the trainees. But I want to reiterate how thorough we are."

"She did," I said as I sipped.

"Anyway, there's what the client wants and there's what the family wants, and often they don't match up at all. There are interventions. That's when you bring in Bethanny. It's best not to take on that kind of turmoil. She's seen it all."

Lorraine's story felt like it was part of a final test. I felt I should be taking notes.

"Do you know what cluster headaches are?"

I shook my head no. She told me about her client Mitchell, who was only thirty-five. It was hard with the young ones, Lorraine told me. She'd had only two clients under the age of forty, but they'd stuck with her.

"They're worse than your worst migraine. Excruciating, consistent pain. Aural hallucinations. Nausea. He would have them for three months straight. Every day. Then he'd have a week or two reprieve before they'd come back again. He tried steroids. Doctors all over the country. Then he came to us."

Mitchell's cluster headaches had gotten so bad that he had ceased getting out of bed, but on the PSAC he was still hovering around 70 percent or 80 percent, depending on who you asked. The pain pills that had once incapacitated him now did nothing. It was his time to go, he decided, and most of his family tacitly supported him. His mother asked if he'd see one more specialist, but he demurred. His family had seen the pain he'd been through, the poking and prodding, the middle-of-the-night heaving and moaning. They often said they didn't know how he had endured this long. Lorraine had brought the family waivers to sign after Bethanny had given her the go-ahead.

"You spend weeks with these clients, getting to know them, making them comfortable, and preparing them to leave us with no regrets and no unfinished business. And through that, you know who is truly ready to go, and who is not."

"It's voluntary," I said.

"That's why we always ask: 'Have all other avenues been explored? Do you understand this is completely voluntary? Do you understand you can opt out anytime?'"

"They have to say they want to die."

"We call it self-deliverance."

"Right," I said, nodding.

Bethanny wanted to make sure that we spent enough time with each client, preparing them for death, so that they—and we—felt confident about their choice. Helping them with all their preparations also took time. Bethanny had considered every last arrangement. Not only did we have to prepare them mentally, but there were technical details to attend to as well. We asked them to assemble lists of all of their passwords to make it easier for those left behind to access bank accounts and anything else they'd have to tidy up afterward. In a way, we were a full-service operation that provided manageable exit plans for people who had no idea of what the aftermath of death could bring.

Lorraine told me that Mitchell was not suicidal per se, but his affliction had reached the point where living with it was unsustainable. He was okay with his choice, and his family, knowing he'd probably find another way—gun or belt—got a referral from a friend.

Lorraine said that when she arrived for her final appointment with Mitchell, his sister was weeping and arranging white lilies while she and another partner wheeled in the helium tank for the hood. It had been on Mitchell to rent the helium tank from a party store. It seemed cruel to make people who were dying wander into a place that catered to vibrant, festive occasions, but we could not risk being detected. We were just a "support mechanism."

Before the final appointment, in addition to administering the questionnaire, and getting from them a list of people they felt they had unfinished business with, or people they felt they had wronged and were ready to make amends to, we also asked them to make amends to themselves, so they could work out any final resentments that they may have been harboring about the way they had lived their own lives. Choices they had made—or regretted not making.

Everything had to be done in order, with the most difficult detachment lessons coming last. Lorraine said she and her partner had done all of this with Mitchell. They even had prepared the letters to be sent to all the people he had listed. They sat with him as he read his own letter of forgiveness to himself.

"We did everything right," she said. "I've helped dozens of people with peaceful transitions."

I wanted to know what Mitchell had forgiven himself for. What he was hoping to get forgiveness from others for. But Lorraine was careful to keep it all private.

"Grief is violent sometimes," Lorraine said. "His sister was beside herself."

I waited for her to give me more, but she just drove me back to my car.

"Anyway, that's not going to be your first time."

She watched a couple around her age slip their arms around each other as they walked along the sidewalk in front of us.

"What happened?" I asked.

"It's just unfortunate. If you get any kind of family push-back, just bring Bethanny in. If she can't talk them down, they can go elsewhere."

She smiled at me and said, "You're going to be meeting your first client soon. If you have questions along the way, just let me know."

I nodded, though I didn't feel remotely ready. But maybe this was the sort of thing you could never be ready for.

"Bethanny's going to send you the client's file in a week or two. I've already started the questionnaire with her, but she wanted to take a break to wind down her treatments."

"What's her name?"

"Daphne."

She leaned over and hugged me again—awkward, because she was wearing her seat belt.

"I'm glad to be doing this with you," she said.

Daphne. I had never met a Daphne before.

11.

It rained for a week straight, long enough for the sound to become familiar again. I still hadn't received Daphne's file, and considered calling or e-mailing Bethanny to tell her that I was anxious and tired of waiting. Though my insomnia had been briefly brought under control during our training sessions, it was back full-force now. Instead of watching juicing infomercials, I got high and read through grief message boards and message boards for women with rare forms of metastatic cancer discussing how many years they had clocked at Stage 4. I don't know what I was looking for, but my lack of sleep was showing on my face in the form of deep pockets under my eyes. I was having a hard time hiding my hangover. I faked a virus and told Bobby I was taking some sick time from work.

One morning, as I checked my e-mail hoping to see Daphne's file, Bobby said, "You still look worn down. When are you going to call the doctor?"

I decided to pay him back by standing up in our marriage counselor's office that evening and screaming, "I don't know how to be a wife."

I wasn't holding my head; my hair wasn't flying out at all sides as if I'd stuck my finger in an electrical socket, like you see in old pictures of unhappy wives. I was wearing jeans and a T-shirt and sneakers that were showing the first signs of a hole at the toe. The doctor was concerned about me. He said, "What part don't you understand? You just have to *be*."

Bobby added, "Why are you acting like it's hard? Just do it. What's the problem?"

We were on month six of counseling because we'd stalled out on the "next steps" stuff—getting a dog, buying a home, having a child. I knew it was my fault, if "fault" was the word. I didn't know what I wanted, but I knew what I didn't want—to wash the dishes, to cook, to clean, to house a fetus, to raise a child. It was becoming a problem.

Jokes were made about simply knocking me up, as in not pulling out in time, on a night when I had had too much to drink. To me, having a child felt like a last gasp of hope for a dying relationship. Nothing's working? *Let's add a baby to the mix.*

It didn't feel like I really had a choice in the matter. Everybody was tapping their toes, waiting for me to snap out of it. At night, I had taken to crossing my arms over my chest and lying very still. Trying to convey, Please don't touch me. It's a funny thing not to trust your husband. To feel like sex was suddenly weaponized.

I still needed my relationships to be radioactive in order for me to feel anything. Yelling, screaming. Flairs for the dramatic meant you really loved me—wanted to fight for me. I have been chased down the street no less than a dozen times by men after a fight, and that was the level of desperation I craved. My mother once told me that when she and my father started dating, she was walking down the hall in their school dorms with another boy. My father asked her who she was walking with when he saw them together, and she told him what she told me: a friend.

"He said, 'If I ever see you walking with him again I'll throw you out this window,'" she told me. "I looked out the window and we were eight floors up."

My mother and I stared at each other and my heart flipped. Imagine someone loving you that much, I thought. Imagine someone needing you that much. I didn't even have to say anything, because she said: "That's how much he loved me."

This is the pitch at which I wanted my love. But Bobby and I had moved from aggression to passive aggression, with underhanded jabs and long silences, and I didn't like that at all.

"Let me ask you something," our therapist said. He was someone we had started making up stories about. Our desire to know what his life was like had temporarily brought us back together. He was slim and often wore short-sleeved button-down shirts that needed to be ironed. Everything else about him, from his glasses to his haircut, was pristine and well manicured. I wondered why he didn't think that a wrinkled shirt collar gave someone the wrong impression about you.

"Okay, let's try this," our therapist said, turning toward me. I didn't like it when he pointed himself at me. He was supposed to remain neutral in his stance, or I thought he should.

"Do you look at relationships through the lens of power or through the lens of love?"

I inhaled and thought about it.

"Power," Bobby said.

"I don't think that about you," I said, gently.

"I'm talking about you."

"I don't."

"Okay."

"Why are you answering for me? I have a voice," I said.

"Why do you think he has the wrong perception of you?" our therapist asked me. I turned my body toward Bobby. We were on opposite sides of the sofa.

"You think I look at relationships through the lens of power?" I asked.

"Yes."

"You seem upset. Do you think it's negative?" our therapist asked me.

"You both make it sound like it is," I said.

"It's a choice," our therapist said.

I looked at Bobby, and he nodded at me like I had just been properly scolded.

"You haven't explained why it's a problem to think that way," I said to our therapist.

"Do you agree it's accurate?" our therapist asked me.

"What relationship isn't about power?" I asked.

Bobby and I had taken separate cars to the therapist's office, our rides to and from becoming increasingly excruciating. After our appointment, I took the long way to my car to think about what power I could give up.

Our marriage counselor was always pushing us into uncomfortable conversations so he could watch us interact and help us move our arguments from unproductive to *productive*. I had wanted to broach the topic of detachment in our session but got derailed by the power conversation. I was so pissed that I wanted to go back into the office and say that I had just done an exercise that showed me that I have very little attachment to anything. What would they have to say about that?

I knew that Bethanny's asking us to make a list of ten things we weren't willing to give up was a standard attachment exercise, a self-help tactic so you realize your attachments to items are a burden rather than adding anything substantial to your life.

I also knew that when you leave someone, there are things you must be willing to give up in your life. Things you bought together and things people gave you as wedding gifts, housewarming gifts, and other markers of progress. I could have told them that what I learned about myself is that I have no problem giving things up.

In fact, I had given up things before. Sofas, beds left in alleyways behind apartments I would never see again, along with people I would never see again.

As I walked to my car, I saw a FOR RENT sign and looked at the building. It was on a busy street, thick vines of green ivy separating the building from the exhaust and cars. I dialed the number on the sign and was surprised when a man picked right up.

"I'm calling about the apartment."

"Are you outside?"

"I am. I wanted to see it."

I felt like I was doing something inappropriate. The first toe dipped into a new life.

"I'll come to the gate," he said.

I hung up and waited for him to come down. He was bald and wearing shorts and a dirty white T-shirt and looked like I had interrupted his afternoon.

"Sorry, I was just calling for an appointment," I said.

"It's fine. I live here."

He brought me up the stairs of the complex, a mid-century

Hollywood standard, with courtyards and small chairs and overgrown indoor houseplants in mismatched planters outside tenants' front steps. Everything had a thin layer of dust on it from the exhaust pumped up from the street.

"Did you just start looking?" he asked.

"Yes."

"We just put the sign up. The apartment is a one-bedroom. It's kind of loud, but what do you expect on this street."

He opened the door to the empty apartment. Our footsteps echoed on the wood floor as he showed me around. The living room was small, but airy. The kitchen was teal-tiled, with the small nooks ubiquitous in apartments of this era. Everything had been painted in white several times over, possibly yearly. It still smelled like the latest coat. As he talked, I ducked from room to room and imagined starting my life over here and what it would feel like, coming home and being alone in it night after night. There were no signs of people in the courtyard, no sounds of them coming from behind the hallway doors. The entire place felt empty, a place you come to live in between other stops in your life.

"Did you just get to Los Angeles?"

"No, I've been here."

"Will you be living alone, then?"

"I think so."

"It's a little small for a couple, but people have done it before."

"I'm not in a couple."

I could see him looking at my wedding ring and I didn't say anything. This apartment wouldn't fit my things, even half of them. I would have to buy everything new, cobble together a life I could make small again—half the size it was now.

Walking through the apartment felt like trying on another

life. I felt like I was cheating by making a big decision without Bobby. But I knew this wasn't going to be my apartment. This was me pushing myself. Could I do it: could I leave yet or not?

Today I couldn't.

12.

When Lorraine finally e-mailed me Daphne's questionnaire, it was from an AOL account and she didn't apologize for the delay. She said they hadn't gotten very far but she wanted to introduce me to Daphne so we could start getting comfortable with each other. Daphne's answer to "Do you believe in God?" didn't illuminate anything new for me. She wrote: "I was brought up Catholic. I had no choice."

Daphne was sixty-four and had Stage 4 cancer, which had moved from her breast to her lungs. It had been lodged in those parts of her for a decade, small and unmoving, but recently the mass decided it had been dormant long enough. Daphne was having trouble walking, heading toward bedridden. She was hovering around 50 or 60 percent on the PSAC, Lorraine told me on our drive to the house.

Daphne lived in one of those ranch homes with wood paneling covering the walls and a pool in the concrete backyard—relaxed, casual, and very California 1970s. She also had a small dog, a beige cocker spaniel named Pierre.

"Pierre's nice, but you have to watch out for his little dickie."

This was one of the first things she said to Lorraine and me after we held the living room in silence for her.

"He likes to get overexcited, and then *watch out*."

"Has he always been like that?" I asked.

"I don't know. He was a rescue."

I leaned down to pet him, and he seemed normal enough. I wondered why Lorraine hadn't warned me in the car on the way over.

Daphne's house was nearly tidy, though evidence of her depleting state was casually strewn about. She had a Styrofoam head with a bobbed wig sitting on a side table like an accessory. Her soft gray hair was shaved short, only an inch or two, but it wasn't patchy. It still looked like a choice. Baggies of coiled plastic tubing from her oxygen machine were piled next to the sofa where she was reclining. Just beyond her were large canisters of emergency oxygen. In case the power went out and she had to go old-school, she told us. I could hear the familiar whizz and click of the oxygen machine she was supposed to be hooked up to, but she didn't have tubes coming out of her nostrils when she talked to us. She noticed me staring at her hair.

"I only realize I'm sick when I pass a mirror," she said.

She told us she just needed a hit of oxygen sometimes; she didn't want to get hooked on it.

"I sleep with it in, though. I'm afraid I'll stop breathing in my sleep."

I told her regulating it was probably the right move.

"If you rely on it too much, then you'll be tied down to a machine, with only a twenty-foot radius to walk in," I said.

"I bet you've seen that with other clients," she said.

I didn't correct her. I just nodded.

She said she liked ambling around her yard and watching Pierre run in circles, chase after squirrels, and dig at the fence, convinced he could overtake the rooster on the other side.

"I hear that thing every morning, as if we're on a farm and not in the suburbs," she said.

The coffee table was strewn with sweated-through to-go cups and empty water bottles. A pile of Jolly Rancher wrappers lay in front of her. She caught me staring.

"I know the forms I filled out say I have diabetes. A side effect of the medication—can you imagine? I don't give a shit."

"I wouldn't, either," I said.

She looked at me and winked. We were on the same team. She eyed Lorraine, sizing her up to see if she should join, too.

"You said last time that you were getting a home-care bed," Lorraine said.

"That's coming. Don't rush me," Daphne said. "They're delivering it next week. Medicare has to approve it. There isn't a fucking thing in my life they don't approve now."

"It's in their best interest to keep people hanging on," Lorraine said.

"They're sapping me of my will to live," Daphne said. "Deliver me upstairs already."

"We have some things to get through first," Lorraine said.

"I know, I know, I know," Daphne said, waving Lorraine away.

Pierre came wagging into the room, and his tail knocked over some empty water bottles.

"Would you mind letting him out?" Daphne asked Lorraine as I hung back and forced myself not to start tidying up the room. Daphne must have sensed it, because she told me she had someone who came once a week.

"Sit down next to me. Your youth is making me nervous."

I did what I was told while Lorraine watched Pierre lift his leg. She averted her eyes when his erection came out in full force.

"The poor thing. He just has an unfortunate tic."

"He's a good boy," I said.

She trained her eyes on me.

"I'm Evelyn," I said, before she could ask.

"Evelyn. Evelyn. What brings you here, Evelyn?"

"You."

Lorraine came back and handed me the questionnaire and pointed to the question they had left off with. She turned on a tape recorder and placed it next to some anesthesia aftercare paperwork that had been thoroughly highlighted and underlined for emphasis.

"Who or what occupies your thoughts most often?" I asked.

"Hospitals," Daphne said.

She told us about the waiting rooms of various cancer centers she had spent time in. How she watched women and men with and without wigs or their natural hair being led in and out of double doors. She knew the drill, but still she couldn't square why she had gotten mixed up with these people. She didn't like to think of herself as a sick person.

"They're very fancy, these cancer centers. You can tell they have money. You should see the art."

She said she watched as one woman in particular, hair newly growing in, walked out of the double doors holding a certificate.

"And what do I do with this now?" the woman asked the nurse who was navigating her back into the waiting room.

Daphne said she watched as the woman's fingers crumpled the edge of the certificate. When she dropped her hand, Daphne said she could see the loops of cursive, the woman's name, Jane, written out in ink on a line in the middle. Like a good-effort certificate one hands out to kindergartners just for showing up, she said.

"You completed the program," the nurse had told Jane.

"My radiation?"

"Yes, you should be proud."

"Is the cancer gone?"

"Cancer goes to sleep, but it's never gone," Daphne told me, breaking from her story.

"I know," I said.

"You know a lot about it. How?" She cut me off before I could divulge anything. "Not my business."

She leaned down to pet Pierre.

"If they gave me that certificate you think I'd hang it on the wall next to my college diplomas? Please." She laughed. "Like I want to remember where I've been."

I stared at her and knew she didn't.

"They ring a bell, too," Daphne said. "The nurse led her over to a gong."

"Why?"

"They wanted her to hit the gong in celebration," Daphne said. "To celebrate her survival."

Daphne said she thought about when she bought her first car from the dealership. How they had a bell to ring, too, so everyone in the dealership could cheer for you and make you feel like you had won something.

"This was winning more time," Daphne told me. "I watched as that woman picked up the mallet. It didn't seem like she wanted to do it, but she also didn't want to disappoint the nurses. So she walked over to the gong, and I could see a light flash in her eyes right before she hit it. Like, in that second she believed she was a winner."

I stared at Daphne as she waved her hand at the absurdity of it all.

"She hit it, though. She hit it as hard as she could and scared the shit out of everyone in the waiting room. Probably took a good year off from all of them. And guess what?"

"What?" I asked.

"The nurses clapped. No one else cheered her on, but the nurses did. Like she was on a fucking game show."

"She must have been happy that she didn't have to come back anymore," I said.

"I hit the gong once," Daphne said, wistfully. "The thing that they don't tell you is that everyone else in that waiting room hates you for getting that certificate. They think you're smug for making a show of it."

"How do you know that?" I asked.

"Because that's how I felt when Jane was doing it. Like she was shoving it in our faces that she was going to live and maybe we weren't. Probably, we weren't going to make it."

"But you hit the gong."

"That was years ago. Look at me now. I don't need awards just for surviving a few extra years."

The idea of a survival gong made me want to burst out laughing. As Daphne rolled her eyes, I wondered why there was no such gong for surviving other life trials—like sustaining a marriage. What would a certificate of achievement look like if you made it one year, two, three, ten? They were not the same thing at all, incurable diseases and marriage, yet for those who found that it didn't come naturally, marriage felt like a sort of improbable accomplishment that needed rewarding.

"How many more do we need to answer today?"

"We can stop if you're tired," Lorraine said.

"Thank you." She pointed at her side table. "I wrote two letters. You can take them."

Lorraine shuffled through her papers and settled on two handwritten letters. She handed them to me.

"We can mail them for you," I said.

"The people are already gone."

"Then we'll keep them safe," Lorraine said.

When we walked back to Lorraine's car, I didn't feel like talking, or processing together. I could tell Lorraine didn't want to, either.

"She's a character," Lorraine said.

"She is."

We drove in silence as Lorraine slowly wended her way through streets the GPS directed her to. To avoid collisions on the freeway, we had ended up north of the city, where horse ranches were abundant. I stared out the window as Lorraine slowed to a crawl so we could look at horses meandering on someone's land. She rolled down her window and stuck her arm out, as if she was hoping she could actually touch them.

"Beautiful," she said. I rolled down my window, too. Eucalyptus trees lined the road around us, pale against the late-afternoon blue sky, and I stared at their peeling trunks and their leaves rustling in the wind. The bright smell of eucalyptus filled the car, and we both inhaled.

"You almost forget you're in Los Angeles," I said.

"I had no idea it could be like this."

When we finally reached the freeway, it was choked with cars heading toward the city, and we both closed the windows.

When we got back to my parked car, Lorraine said she'd give me a few days to journal and then she'd check in.

"They don't get easier, is the problem," she said.

"I wouldn't expect them to."

"Good."

I realized I was still holding Daphne's letters when Lorraine drove away.

THE BEST TIME TO GO to a bar is right when it opens. Around 5:00 p.m. They're usually mostly empty, and you can be nearly alone to drink for at least an hour before happy-hour people start to arrive. You also always look like you're waiting for someone, so no one can ever really accuse you of having a problem.

There are those kinds of bars, and then there are the kinds of bars that open at 6:00 a.m. and close at 2:00 a.m., leaving approximately four hours for the casual alcoholic to have to go find somewhere else to sit. I had spent the better part of my twenties in the latter, but they didn't have the same kind of pull anymore.

Still, I found myself parking in front of one such bar, the beckoning yellow sign weak now. The door was heavy and the interior was just as I remembered it: dark like a tomb and thick with the smell of decades of stale beer. The light from outside always jarred alert whoever was hovering over their drink at the bar. Several men turned to look at me briefly and then went back to nursing. I looked through my wallet and found twenty-six dollars. I asked for tequila neat and knew I could stretch my money to cover three drinks if I asked for well liquor.

I took a seat in a vinyl booth closest to the jukebox, so I could get some light from the glow, and opened the first of Daphne's letters.

To her mother, Daphne kept things short, shorter than what I would have written to my own mother. Mostly memories of summers at the beach near Santa Monica Pier, a genuine thank-you for letting her stay out past curfew on summer nights to stroll along the beach and boardwalk with her boyfriend. She recounted that first flush of excitement as they walked along the cliffs in the Palisades and spied the lights of the pier glittering in a line against the dark water. How she clutched her boyfriend's hand in joy and had never forgotten that warmth, the coarseness of his fingers and palms from working with horses in the Santa Monica Mountains. How they lost touch when she went to college, but she never forgot him or that summer. She thanked her mother for letting her become a woman with ease, despite her father's desire that she stay a good and moral girl.

But her letter to her father was different. He appeared, from her writing, to be a brutal man—and one that she was having trouble forgiving. He was a sober alcoholic, which she pointed out was almost worse, because he couldn't contain his fury at not being able to drink. And so the family dealt with the ebbs and flows of his moods—his rage, really—and Daphne outlined it all back to him. Brutal fathers were hard to shake as you moved through life. It was more acute for daughters, it seemed, because fathers were our models for how men should treat us. I finished my tequila and ordered another, this time asking for two limes.

There is a theory in self-help circles that a certain early relationship dynamic imprints onto you and you seek to play out that dynamic with each new mate you let into your life, hoping for a different outcome each time. Think of it as a sort of do-over but you keep making the same mistakes. For instance, watching my mother trying to love my father enough to make him happy—to save him from himself—imprinted onto me as the proper way to love someone. Over the course of my own relationships, I had replayed this dynamic with my own emotionally unavailable men and destroyed myself in the process. With the men I consistently chose, Bobby included, I had been the strong one.

But I also now knew that being with men who were emotionally unavailable meant I could be emotionally unavailable, too. In fact, I could be just as emotionally unavailable as they were while pretending I was *giving it my all*. And when Bobby or anyone else would confront me by saying, "You always seem like you have one foot out the door," I would say, "I'm all in. And you're not." Or, "I only seem that way because you make me feel unsafe—like you're going to leave, so I want to get the jump."

Bobby once called me an emotional terrorist. In turn, I told him he was a willing victim. It was not always like this. We fell for each other like normal people. There was texting. There was excitement and nervousness about having sex for the first time. There were the days after, when I couldn't quite think straight because all I did was replay every moment we spent together. I could smell his cologne even when he wasn't with me. The first time we had sex, I didn't shower for two days so I could still smell his sweat on me. Maybe I was veering into obsession, but what I felt for him was more intense than anything I had ever felt before, and I found it both extremely uncomfortable and supremely exhilarating.

I wouldn't eat unless I received a text from him, because trying to find hunger in the absence of communication was impossible. My shoulders became sharp and angular. We moved in together three months after we met, because it hurt to be apart.

I KNEW I HAD TO LEAVE the bar when I ran out of money and didn't have the wherewithal to have an incoherent talk with a man who had been here for hours, in hopes that he'd buy me more.

I went outside and stared at the bright blue of dusk. The moon was already steady above me.

When I got home from the bar, Bobby wasn't home. I called my mother and told her I wanted to separate. I wasn't drunk exactly, but I had a little more courage.

At first, she was very quiet, and then she said, "Have you tried everything?"

I had never heard her voice sound so flat. She had been angry with me many times before, even hurt. But this was different. This was defeat. Or maybe I was the one conveying defeat and she was just trying to be supportive. She wanted me to list the things I had tried, so she—a woman who had been married for forty-five years—could gauge if I had done enough. Or if I could be convinced to go in for another round. She wanted to be my coach, I could tell.

Leaving a marriage was serious, she told me. Was I even sure?

My mother wanted to know what I thought I was looking for. That was always the question. What *did* I think I was looking for? What did I want? Whether it was hurtled at me during a fight with Bobby, or asked of me by someone whose life wasn't defined by the answer, at thirty-seven years old I still couldn't say. The question always felt like an indictment, as in *What do you even want?* I knew what I didn't want, but that wasn't the same thing at all.

13.

Even though I was anxious about helping Daphne die, I still wasn't ready to tell Bobby the full truth of what I was doing. It felt like it belonged to a new part of my life and I wanted it to be just mine.

I saw Bethanny's name flash on my phone, and I went to the bathroom to pick it up. She told me Lorraine had to cover a client who needed more support than their current exit guide could supply.

"I can wait for Lorraine to finish if Daphne can," I said.

"Daphne doesn't want to wait. She asked for someone else to take over so she can stay on schedule."

"Okay," I said.

"I also worry Lorraine is having a hard time working with Daphne. She didn't say it, but sometimes it's hard to detach when the person you're helping is a mirror."

Bethanny liked to speak in koans. Sometimes I understood them; sometimes I just wrote them down for later, when I might be able to understand them better.

"Maybe I could talk to her."

"Is this pain avoidance?" Bethanny asked.

"I'm not sure. I'm still struggling with detachment."

"You're stronger than you think," she said. "I've already called Nathan, and he's agreed to take Lorraine's place."

"Permanently?"

"I don't want to destabilize her with changing her guides over and over. Would you prefer I do it with you?"

"No, Nathan's fine," I said.

DAPHNE WAS DYING in the spring. Reports had come out that because of the rare heavy rains that had finally settled over Southern California we were experiencing an April super-bloom that had not been witnessed in at least a dozen years. Meteorologists talked about "atmospheric rivers" with a giddiness I had never seen before. There had even been thunderstorms with hundreds of pulses of lightning per minute shooting down over the Pacific. Bobby told me one thunderbolt had hit a palm tree near our apartment and set it ablaze. People had crowded around it to take pictures instead of calling the fire department. He shook his head while he said it. Purple and yellow flowers crowded the hills around the city, and if you looked closely enough you could see tall grass undulating in the breeze up there, too. The desert, meanwhile, was covered in an array of wildflowers. Cacti were sprouting bright pink and magenta blooms from every direction. For the first time in years, after we'd been living with persistent drought, things were starting to feel verdant again.

Daphne lived near fields where vibrant California poppies bloomed in vast blankets each spring. Each year, for a brief few weeks, cars traveled in packs just for a chance to glimpse the rolling hills of orangey gold. For a couple dollars you could walk through the poppy fields and be transported into a kind of Technicolor dream, as long as you averted your eyes from the thick yellow smog settling over the tract homes in the valley down below. Hordes of people photographed themselves in the sea of flowers and didn't care what they were trampling.

Bobby hated crowds and refused to go see the poppies with me. I wanted to stop to see them the first time I went to meet Daphne. I had mapped it out for my drive with Lorraine. The bloom was only ten miles from Daphne's, and I figured on our next drive we could take the long way past the flowers, since she seemed open to exploration.

But with Nathan, I felt too shy to ask. I didn't know what he looked for in a partner, and asking him for anything that took us off task seemed inappropriate. So far the span of our conversations had not lasted more than a total of six minutes since our pain exercise.

Nathan called me on a Friday. When I saw an 818 number flashing that evening, I did not answer. He left a message suggesting we should meet in a Starbucks parking lot near where Bethanny's sessions took place. I waited ten minutes and texted him back, *Starbucks is great. I'll meet you at 2.*

I waited for dots to appear, my palms starting to sweat a little. A green text box appeared instead: *Cool. Can you call me though?*

I exhaled. I didn't like talking to people on the phone, really. Calling someone out of the blue felt like an intrusion—too intimate—and when I did answer my phone I always sounded surprised, as if I didn't quite know what was happening.

When I called him back, he was engaged without necessarily being warm. It was clear we were still strangers. He said Bethanny had talked to Daphne first and he thought it would be good for me to follow up with her, too, since we were in the process of building our own relationship.

When I called Daphne, she asked, "Is he cute?"

"He's not bad to look at," I said.

"Is he the type of person you wouldn't mind being the last person you see on earth?"

"I wouldn't be mad about it."

"Fair enough."

"He's nice."

"Maybe I can get him to hold my only breast while I take my last breath," she said. "Joking."

She giggled and so did I.

"Put in a good word for me?" she asked.

"I'm not sure how to bring that up, exactly: Can you sexually harass Daphne?"

"There has to be an extra-services clause somewhere," she said, laughing. "Final wishes?"

"You might change your mind after you see him," I said. "Maybe he's not your type."

"At this point everyone's my type," she said.

We laughed together, but a slight depression was starting to wedge its way under my skin. It didn't feel fair that she could be this sharp while physically deteriorating.

"Anyway, he has to be better than that other one," she said.

"Lorraine?"

"Totally humorless."

"She's okay when you get to know her."

"At least you pretend you care."

"She's focused on detachment."

I rummaged through my purse absentmindedly while we talked and found my prescription refills. One for Klonopin, one for Xanax. The Xanax pills were oblong and white, and bitter when I chewed on them. The Klonopin pills, meanwhile, were pink and perfect circles. They tasted sweet, and each had a line in the middle to demarcate half-doses. I pulled them out of the pharmacy bag and lined them up on my dining table. I pulled out the old bottles, which still had half a dozen of each pill inside.

"I appreciate what you're doing. I don't want to do it alone."

I wanted to say: *I don't want you to do it at all.*

I opened the pill bottles and went about consolidating each set.

"What are you doing?" Daphne asked.

I paused. I wasn't sure if I should lie.

"I'm consolidating my anxiety medication," I said quietly.

She burst out laughing.

"I didn't think you could hear me."

"I know the rattle of pill bottles!"

"I just got my refills," I said, embarrassed.

"I'll round mine up so you can have them after I go," she said.

"Only the good ones."

"Not the cancer medication. Too toxic," she said. "The nurses have to wear gloves when they hand me the pill. And then I put it in my mouth."

I stifled a sound.

"See you tomorrow, I guess," Daphne said.

We weren't supposed to get attached, but I could feel myself *going there* with Daphne. We weren't supposed to have opinions on the deaths of our clients. In a way, we were simply service workers. Here to give the clients what they wanted.

Nathan met me at the Starbucks and we both ordered coffees—he ordered a Mocha Frappuccino, which I thought was weird, because he seemed like a person who cared about what he put in his body—and I trailed him to his car, scanning the parking lot filled almost entirely with white cars. I wasn't sure what I was expecting, but he had an anonymous slate-gray Prius, one of thousands zipping around Los Angeles.

"I can drive," he said.

"Great," I said, thinking of the poppy fields and how I might bring them up.

Nathan didn't know which surface streets and sneaky routes to take to avoid sitting in congestion. We sat in traffic on the 5 Freeway almost all the way up to Six Flags. Nathan wanted to talk about Daphne and her exit. He wanted to know if she was in good spirits during our follow-up call, and I considered telling him about her breast request, but thought it was too soon. Also, there was a chance she might just ask him herself.

After we ran out of Daphne things to discuss, I asked, "Why do you do this?"

"My father," he said. "I hated watching him die. I thought there had to be a better way."

He looked at me, though he wasn't expecting a response. We had been through the same program and we weren't victims of our circumstances anymore.

"Why do you?"

"I'm preparing myself for the people I love."

"Oh yeah, there are a lot of people like you who come to Bethanny," he said.

I felt like I was on the opposite side of some giant divide: someone who was still untouched by the kind of catatonic grief that comes with having a parent die. No amount of preparation was going to help me. I just wanted to be less leveled.

"Where is she on the PSAC?"

"Hovering around sixty percent," I said. "She's very lucid. It's disconcerting."

"What do you mean?" Nathan asked.

"It almost seems like she could get better."

"She's Stage Four. There's no Stage Five."

"Some people live at Stage Four for a long time."

"She already has."

"I just mean that she still has some time. It's not like she's dancing around her house, but you know."

"People have different thresholds. What's yours?"

"I think I wrote down fifty percent. But it's honestly more like seventy."

"Seventy percent is barely showing signs of sickness," he said, and laughed.

"I don't really have a strong will to live."

"Dark."

"I'm not a depressed person," I said, weirdly defensive. "What are you, at twenty percent?"

"This process is difficult."

"I'm saying there are people who have lost their will to live, and she's not one of them."

"You," he said.

"Yes, she definitely wants to live more than I do."

"She doesn't, though. And that's her choice," he said, changing lanes.

"I get it," I said. "She called us, not the other way around."

"What'd you do before this?" he asked.

I worked behind counters, at registers, or as a secretary. Secretarial work felt the most substantial, because it carried with it the promise of health insurance and retirement plans if you chose to be a lifer. The offices I had worked in were full of lifers: women who had slid behind their desks in their early twenties and hadn't moved, well into their fifties and sixties. In these offices, you became a person who decorated your desk with years of pictures of momentous life occasions and jars of candy used to lure people for daytime breaks in between stringing calls together and maintaining complicated appointment calendars for someone else, while barely being able to handle your own affairs. All I could look back at were jobs that didn't really matter—ones that were always just going to be *jobs*—while everyone around me settled into *careers*, doing things they found fulfilling.

I worked in places where I was asked if I knew how to write a cover letter, even though I had been through four years of college and could most certainly pull out a "To Whom It May Concern." I wasn't going to get into all that with Nathan. I didn't want to start at a deficit.

"Random stuff. It doesn't matter," I said. "What about you?"

"I was an IT manager."

"What is that, even?"

"You don't know what an IT manager is?"

"I'm not being rude. People say it all the time, but what does it mean? It just sounds impressive."

I wasn't sure he was buying my attempt to save the conversation, but I refused to look him in the face to check.

"Well, my boss had no idea how to use her computer, so I would travel around with her on her business trips to make sure she could access her e-mails. I'd also check the Wi-Fi in the office. I made it look hard. Before that I was an apartment manager."

"Really?"

"Is that more or less impressive? I can't tell," he said.

I looked at him, and he was smirking.

"Free rent is impressive."

"It was a high point."

"Did you evict people?"

"It made me feel awful to do it."

"So now you're making amends?" I asked.

"Something like that. I've found spirituality through this work. My way of building up better karma."

"A bonus," I said.

After a brief silence he asked, "How many times have you seen Daphne?"

"Just once, but I've read her letters," I said.

"And her pain?"

"She's no longer avoiding it."

"I could see why you'd like her," he said, and suddenly we were at Daphne's house.

14.

Daphne had texted me that she had told her nurse to leave the door unlocked and she would be in bed when we arrived. *I'm tired today*, she texted. Nathan asked me to go inside first and I appreciated that.

"How are you feeling, Daphne?" he asked, standing next to her bed.

"As well as can be expected," she replied, looking Nathan up and down.

He gathered an armful of her cups that were scattered on her bedside table.

"My nurse can clean those up," she said. "Before I fire her next week."

"It's no problem," Nathan said, before heading to the kitchen.

"Where's Pierre?" I asked.

"You only came over here to see Pierre? I'm the one who needs you."

She looked at me and winked. All I wanted to do was tell her how much I needed her.

"I don't care about Pierre at all," I said, sitting down on the edge of her bed.

"He's going to be heartbroken when I tell him. He's staying

with a friend. I'm trying to see who he might want to live with when I'm gone. I don't want him to end up in a kill shelter, because he's a little weird."

I thought about who would want to take on a dog with a constant erection.

"I don't think you could handle him," Daphne said. "I see how you look at him. But he's very particular about the company he keeps."

"I could take care of him," I said. I didn't really want to, but I wanted Daphne to think of me as someone she could trust with something she loved.

"Pierre would have to do a trial run with you first to see. A weekend. But I guess it's too late in the game for that. You should have come around sooner."

"I'd be happy to dog-sit him at my place."

"What will your husband say?" she asked, pointing to my wedding ring.

"He won't mind," I lied.

"I'll think about it. Let me talk to Pierre."

When she held up her arm, her flesh hung low and crinkled. I hadn't noticed how thin she was. But who I saw in her bed compared with the photos that lined her living room walls was a shock that was hard to hide.

"I look bad, don't I?"

"No, not at all."

"My skin is crepey and I hate it. It makes me look so old. I'm not old. I just lost muscle mass."

"I know you're not old, Daphne."

"That's what's so dumb about this. My body is failing, but up here—up here—I'm perfect."

She pointed at her head, and what was happening to her felt exceptionally cruel to me.

"You know cancer tricks your brain into thinking you're not hungry? It wants you to starve."

"I didn't," I said, feeling breathless for a moment.

"Everyone out there is golfing. I'm trapped in here, in this body," she said.

She swung her arm again, and I took her body in. She looked so small. She had worn a billowy shirt with long sleeves during our previous visit, so this was the first time I fully saw what the disease had done to her.

"I never fucking liked golf anyway."

She smiled, and I laughed so I wouldn't do anything to embarrass myself like weep—which was totally unprofessional. Nathan came back into the bedroom, wiping his hands on his pants.

"What's so funny?" he asked.

"Evelyn told me you were handsome, and I was just thanking her for the heads-up. I put on some blush, did you notice?"

I blushed, but Nathan moved past me, totally focused on Daphne.

"Very pretty," he said. I didn't want to be the one to ask about the breast, and I wasn't sure if Daphne had the nerve.

"You're making me want to reconsider," Daphne said, winking at Nathan.

"You know I'm going to have to report that, don't you?" he said. "Because you can opt out anytime. I hope you know that."

"It was off the cuff," she said. "I still want to get out of here. Next life's gotta be better."

"Have you decided which way you'd like to go, then?" I asked.

"The hood seems a little gruesome. I think I'll go the cupful-of-Seconal route."

I looked at Nathan, who nodded to me.

"How can we make you more comfortable, Daphne?" he asked.

"Just stand in the light so I can get a really good look at you," she said, making Nathan laugh.

"She and I are turning the tables. Sexually harassing *you*. Feminism taken to its natural next step," she said.

He looked at me, bemused, and I tried to hide my mortification.

"Looks like I should give you two a minute," I said.

"Oh no, can't trust us alone," she said. "Last kicks."

"Or I could leave you two alone and you could continue plotting," he said.

"No plotting here. Just having some fun before I go. Let me have that, won't you?"

"Of course," he said. "Whatever you want."

"I don't think you're prepared to give me what I want."

She tapped him on the arm and he laughed.

"One last thing," Daphne said. "I haven't been able to drink citrus because of this medication—sores in my mouth, I don't need to give you a visual. And I'm not supposed to drink alcohol—drug interactions and all that. But I don't give a damn about the pain if it's my last drink. I want you to make it taste like a Tequila Sunrise."

"I'm not sure I know how to make that," Nathan said.

"Better learn quick."

"That reminds me. Have you filled out the last part of your paperwork?" Nathan asked.

"What did I have left?"

"Funeral arrangements."

"No, but I know what I want."

"I'm going to use the bathroom," I said.

"It's probably a mess. I don't want any flowers. I want everyone who comes to the funeral to send money to the equestrian center instead."

"I don't mind," I said.

"We can do that," Nathan said. He took out a binder and a pen as I left the room.

I walked down the hallway toward the bathroom, and a pungent smell in the air hit me. It was a mix of urine and other body smells, which enveloped me as I closed the bathroom door. I looked down and saw that the trash was full of used adult diapers. Her bathtub was grimy and housed a slumped mop that looked like it hadn't been moved in weeks. I leaned down and pulled the bag out of the trash and tied it up, upset that her nurse wasn't taking better care of her. I left the bag on the floor while I peed, the toilet bowl filthy with brown specks around the rim. I was angry with myself for humiliating her by needing to go to the bathroom. I was worried she would say something to me that would make us both feel awkward, so I quietly went outside and avoided going anywhere near where she was lying down.

I took the bag outside and threw it in the trash next to her house. Nathan came up behind me and said, "I see what you mean about her."

"I didn't tell her you were handsome," I said.

"It's okay if you did."

We were staring at the flower-covered hills beyond Daphne's house, and Nathan was trying to call the main office to see if we had enough pills. She had originally requested the hood, and her change of heart meant we had to scramble to stay close to her schedule. I stared at the one large vein curving around Nathan's forearm; his arm muscles weren't oversized, but somehow they all fit into a not-so-slight package. We went back inside and told Daphne it would take up to ten days to collect all the Seconal. She did not say no to the timing or try to cancel. Instead, she took my hand and said, "Great." She looked around her bedroom. "I need you to do something else for me."

"Whatever you need," I said.

"I bought pants and a jacket from Ann Taylor, and I need you to send them back for me."

"What?"

"I don't know why I bought them. I don't need them. Take a look, maybe you want them for yourself."

She motioned toward a shipping bag, and I went and pulled the items out.

"I like this jacket," I said.

"Do you want it?"

It was a knit jacket that looked like the kind of thing marketed to mature women—a Chanel knockoff. I shook my head no.

"Do you think I should wear it to my funeral?"

"Like, in the casket?"

"I won't need that jacket in heaven."

"It's tasteful," I said, holding it up. The color suited her, and I could tell she was considering it.

"Just put it in the mail. I already filled out the return slip."

NATHAN AND I DROVE AWAY from her house in silence, and I didn't hear from him again until two days later, when he called to ask how I was doing and if I wanted to carpool again when the time came for Daphne's appointment. I said fine to both. It seemed like he wanted to ask me something else, but he didn't, and I didn't push.

I took Daphne's package to the post office and focused on fulfilling other mundane errands. I didn't tell Bobby about the carpool situation or about the dog or even what was about to happen to Daphne. It felt slightly transgressive, perhaps because I wanted it to be.

Bobby had taken to meditating for long hours at a time. Meditating on being present, he told me. You could say we were growing apart. Instead of "working on our marriage," as our therapist had told us to do—by spending more time together, getting out of the script of our lives, and doing spontaneous things—I devoted most of my free time to continuing to study Bethanny's training materials, so I could feel absolutely prepared for what was about to happen. So far it was not going very well. I also wanted to call Daphne and ask her how she'd kept it going for sixty-four years.

Tell me anything that can help me do this, I wanted to beg her, *how to live this life*. I made a pact with myself to ask her just before she passed, even though this definitely fell under "making the death about yourself."

Daphne called me the next day about Pierre.

"My friend is going to keep him," she said.

"I understand."

"You're disappointed. I can hear it in your voice. But there are shelters full of dogs who need a good home."

"I know, I know."

"You had your heart set on Pierre."

"I didn't, really."

"I'll give your name and number as a backup in case something happens."

"You don't have to do that."

"You can be an emergency contact. It's what Pierre would want."

"Daphne, I don't need to be."

"You can handle it. I wanted to tell you in case his new owner calls you with *an emergency*."

"Is there something you want to do before your final appointment?" I asked her.

"Like what?"

"I don't know. Go to a restaurant you like or something."

"Last meal."

"Not that grim."

"There's a place I used to go in the Valley when I was young that I wouldn't mind visiting again."

"I'll take you there."

"Is that allowed?"

"I won't tell anyone if you don't."

"I love secrets," she said. "Let's do it."

The next few days felt excruciatingly long.

I did the normal things—the ones that made you feel like an adult who was also part of a network of adults committed to doing the same thing over and over again. Like going to the grocery store.

The parking lot was always jammed full of impatient people waiting for their turn to slide into compact parking spots before slamming their doors into the sides of the cars next to them. And once that was sorted, we struggled with shopping carts that became increasingly impossible to navigate through hordes of people trying to get the last box of spaghetti or bag of lentils. Whatever it was, we would all fight over it. Instead of fighting, I lingered in the wine aisle, which was usually the most relaxed aisle, trying to decide if I could splurge on eight-dollar wine or if I'd need to stick to the $5.99 selection I had grown tired of. But I couldn't come home with a cartful of wine, so I dragged myself through other aisles, wishing there was a pill you could take for nutrients rather than always having to do this.

I also did laundry. I sat in the backyard with a drink while I waited for the machines to do their thing. The light in the back of our apartment building had burned out months ago, and so I sat in the darkness, breathing in the smells of night-blooming jasmine and orange trees with bright white flower buds. The night smells of L.A. are what get you, charm you, and make it feel impossible ever to leave. I thought about Daphne as I sat in the darkness and tried to understand why I was trying to avoid the loss of her. We were supposed to be learning detachment. I knew she was dying, with my help or not, and yet I wanted to prolong her suffering—so I could visit her once a week and learn something from her. People say watching someone pass on will inevitably make you look at your own life and question if you are making the best use of it. I was using Daphne as a clarifier for my life, because I couldn't trust myself to know what I wanted otherwise. Through her letters I could tell she had wished she had been a more active participant in her own.

Bobby was lying on the couch, watching TV, when I came back inside with the laundry.

"I thought you weren't coming back."

He said this more often now, and I took it as a dare.

"I was doing laundry."

"I know, but, like, you don't have to sit outside for two hours."

"I know I don't."

"Did you go to your support group today?" he asked me in an attempt to be conciliatory.

"What are you talking about?"

"Aren't you still going to your support group for grief?"

"I graduated."

"To what?"

"To not having to go anymore."

"You don't always have to be like this."

I nodded, because he was right, but I wanted something I said to be the final straw for him, so I didn't have to make the decision.

"I think I'm going to go out and see some friends tomorrow night," he said.

"Sounds good."

Instead of telling him I was going out with Daphne, I said I had a spin class.

"Do you want to know who?" he asked.

"Tell me or don't," I said.

"Tell me or don't" was not what he wanted to hear. This was our script, and it soon spiraled into familiar territory, which ended in his sleeping on the couch and my staring at the ceiling alone in our bedroom. My first instinct was usually to fix, to make him happy, to take it back, and also to berate myself quietly for being a broken person who could not be a productive part of a unit. But this time I didn't do any of those things.

15.

The place Daphne wanted me to take her was in a part of the Valley I had never been to before. She used to go there in its heyday, and she heard it was closing. She wanted to see it one last time. It was the kind of nondescript mid-century bar you could find in parts of Los Angeles that had escaped redevelopment, the neon signs often the most interesting part. The bright neon sign above us cast a strange light on Daphne. She was wearing her wig and she looked like a different person. She kept touching it as if she was surprised to find it there, too. The light made the grooves that had gathered along her cheeks seem deeper and more severe; the shimmery blush Daphne had asked me to apply before we left her house suddenly looked clownish. As we walked up to the place she asked, "How do I look?"

"Beautiful."

She clutched my arm as I crossed the sidewalk, and I could tell she walked with hesitation. She asked me to hold her bag and I asked her why it felt so heavy.

"My oxygen concentrator."

She played with the zipper to get the bag open, and I saw the machine in there, turned off, the familiar clear tubing coiled around it.

This field trip felt dangerous all of a sudden.

"They used to serve dinner here," she said.

"Are you hungry?"

"No, I'm just giving you the history."

I opened the door and I could see those days had passed. Inside, the booths were green Naugahyde and the carpet a psychedelic pattern that must have been from the sixties. It had been trapping the smell of stale beer and cigarette smoke ever since. Daphne surveyed the bar, the pictures on the wall that told the place's story. Black-and-white photos of people dressed in suits and fitted dresses showed what kind of place this used to be. Once a place you came to show off, now it just had a handful of old drunks lining the bar. The bartender, an older Filipina, nodded at us but didn't say hello.

The men who kept vying for the bartender's attention didn't register us at all.

"Where do you want to sit?"

"That booth. It was my booth."

She clutched her purse as she made her way past the barstools and into her booth. Making a move to sit down, she fell onto the Naugahyde in a way that worried me.

"Are you okay?"

"I just lost my balance for a second. Get me a drink, honey."

"Sure, of course. What do you want?"

"Tequila, maybe. What do they have?"

She scanned the bar. I could see a row of different Pucker and schnapps bottles. Low-shelf liquor. I wanted to take her somewhere better. Somewhere fancy and classy, to get a martini, a final memory that could compete with her original.

"You know what I used to drink here? Midori Sours."

"You want a Midori Sour? What about your mouth sores?"

"Forget them. Tell the bartender to make it with Cointreau."

I walked up to the bartender and sat down next to an old man hunched over his drink and a crossword puzzle.

"What are you ladies having?"

"She wants a Midori Sour, but make it with Cointreau. And I'll just have a tequila soda."

"We have Triple Sec."

I turned to check with her and saw her peering at the pictures on the wall and smiling.

"That's probably fine."

I took out my credit card, and the bartender shook her head.

"Cash only."

She pointed to the ATM. I could ask Daphne for money or I could see how much was left in my bank account. I took out forty dollars from the ATM and stared at my last hundred dollars in checking. My 401(k) money had not yet hit my account. I hoped Daphne wasn't in the mood to have more than two drinks.

When I brought the drinks back to our table, she clapped her hands.

"I love that unnatural color. It makes me feel like we're on an island somewhere. Anywhere but here."

Although there was no chance of Bethanny's coming into this particular bar, I still felt anxiety about what we were doing. I knew I wasn't fully in command of the situation while outside of Daphne's home—there were variables I couldn't control—and all I could think about was getting her home at the end of the night.

She moved her drink across the table toward me and smiled. I took a sip and nodded.

"Melon. Yum."

"You don't have to pretend. You won't hurt my feelings."

When I gave it back to her, she took a long sip, then held her cheek.

"Maybe I'll just have the one," she said.

She winced through a smile.

"It sucks getting old. Don't do it," she told me.

"I'm on the fence."

"It doesn't get better than where you're at right now."

"That's not really comforting."

"I spent so many nights here looking for trouble. You don't even know."

I asked her to tell me the stories.

"I could have been any one of these young girls in the pictures. Except I was prettier. And more wild. This place used to be packed with people. And dressed like you wouldn't believe. They're probably all gone now. Or maybe they're all doing great."

"They probably moved to Florida."

"They didn't change the carpets. They haven't changed a thing. It's exactly as I remember it."

She turned around and looked past the jukebox to the hallway.

"What I did in that bathroom!"

She leaned back in the booth and laughed.

"Tell me about your father," I said to her.

She looked at me, confused.

"My father?"

"Yeah, what was he like? What was your relationship like?"

Daphne sighed and looked at the wall for a little while.

"I don't know. What can I say? I wish he loved himself enough to know how to love me."

She looked at me and took a sip of her drink. I didn't know how to answer that. It wasn't a question.

She looked at me like, *Those weren't the kind of memories I came here to have.* So I just sat quietly while she drank.

"You want me to tell you about some big epiphany, don't you?" Daphne asked.

"No. I don't know. Unless you have one?"

"I don't, really. I'm just a person."

"I know. I'm sorry. We can talk about something else."

"Look, when you're my age, there's nothing to look forward to anymore, so you spend all your time looking back. Memories that feel good and ones that don't. You know how much time lately I've spent wishing I could change the past? All of it. All my time sitting in bed is thinking about missed opportunities. But that's all we have—all our missed opportunities to look back on. Why don't you think about that?"

I was worried she was angry with me, so I stared down at my drink.

"I've noticed something about you. You have an eye-contact problem," she said.

"I look at people."

"I think I read somewhere that being bad at eye contact means you're dishonest."

"I don't think I'm dishonest. I'm just scared."

"People want someone to pay attention to them and what they're saying."

"Looking someone in the eye for too long feels like the start of an anxiety attack."

She leaned back and stared at me.

"No one actually wants to hurt you, Evelyn."

I could let out a sob, or I could gulp down my drink to stifle it. I chose the latter and looked away. She wasn't asking me for a staring contest—or, at least, I didn't want to give her one.

She took a long sip of her drink.

"My doctor told me my lungs are weeping. Isn't that a beautiful way of putting it? But they're weeping so much that I'm drowning."

It was her turn to look away.

"Okay, let's go," she said.

She slid across the booth and flipped her legs out to get up. She got up quickly and took a step and fell before I could stop her.

"Daphne!"

I pushed myself out of the booth and crouched next to her. Some of the men craned their necks to see what was happening.

She was already trying to get up.

"I'm sorry," she said.

"Don't be sorry."

"My foot fell asleep, I think. Or it got caught. I don't know what happened. I couldn't feel it anymore."

I helped her up and put her back in the booth.

"Do you need your oxygen?"

"No. Just stay with me."

The bartender came over to see what was happening. She asked us if we needed ice. She went back behind the bar, annoyed, and shoveled ice into a bag.

"She doesn't have to," Daphne said.

I could see her ankle was already swelling.

"I don't think you're going to be able to walk like that."

"It just fell asleep."

"Does it hurt?"

She tried to get up from the booth and had a hard time balancing, so I helped her back down.

"Yes," she said.

She could see my look of concern and said, "We're not going to the hospital. And I don't want to cause a scene, so don't you dare call an ambulance."

"I won't. She's just bringing some ice."

The bartender came back and I put the ice on Daphne's ankle. Blue veins crisscrossed her wrinkled skin, and I noticed she had put on a pair of sparkly sandals for the occasion. Her pants looked pressed and new.

"These shoes were a bad idea," she said. "I just wanted to look nice."

She took the ice pack from me and held it on her ankle herself.

"Is she all right?" the bartender asked me.

"I'm right here and I'm fine."

I looked up at the men staring at us and put up my hands.

"I can't take her anywhere," I said trying to break the tension, but nobody laughed. They stared at me and I stared at Daphne, who looked small and fragile. She looked up at me with confusion and I instantly understood that it was the wrong thing to say.

"I want to go home," she said.

I helped her up and asked her to put her weight on me.

We drove home. Instead of talking, I worried I would have to tell Bethanny what I had done. I helped Daphne into the house, and she asked me to get her a Vicodin, her inhaler, and water. When I asked her if she needed help getting into bed, she waved me away. She wedged the ice next to her ankle and slid into bed with her makeup still on.

"I'm fine, Evelyn," she said. "Go home to your life."

16.

I called Daphne the next morning and asked her if she needed anything. She told me that she was fine and her ankle was only a little bit swollen now. She said she'd told her nurse that she had fallen in her house.

She kept our conversation short, and I assumed that she blamed me for what had happened. She told me she hated being pitied.

"No one wants to feel someone else's regrets," she said.

I couldn't argue with this, so I didn't.

She also said that what happened had only strengthened her resolve about what she was doing. She didn't even sound angry about it, or resigned. She was just matter-of-fact.

She told me she would see me in a few days and hung up.

ON THE DAY I was supposed to meet Nathan to be with Daphne to help her die, I arrived at the Starbucks fifteen minutes early. I didn't want to get all worked up when I saw Daphne, so I took a Xanax as soon as I got in the car.

In the parking lot of Starbucks, waiting for Nathan, I used the rearview to put on lipstick. Red, which I thought might make Daphne a little bit happy. Nathan caught me putting the finishing touches on my lipstick, and it occurred to me that he might think the flourish was for him. That was partially true, but I didn't want him giving himself all the credit.

"Do you want to drive?" he asked, leaning in through my window.

"Sure," I said.

"My car's been acting funny, and I don't want it to overheat on the way there and mess everything up."

I looked around my car, not having anticipated a passenger. He slid in and I handed him the directions. I took off, heading to the 5 as he paged through them. He was in my car, and I was suddenly worried that it might smell, like I had become immune to the pile of shoes I kept hidden in the hatchback trunk, and they might still be pungent to newcomers. Once on the freeway, I turned up the A/C.

"How was your week?" Nathan asked.

"It was weird. I didn't feel impending doom or anything, but everything just slowed down. But now we're here."

I wasn't about to tell him what had happened to Daphne. I didn't want to get kicked out of the program.

"Does each person affect you differently?" I asked.

"Yeah. But I write down details from each one in here," he said, pulling out a small notebook. "Because I don't want to forget."

"Do you take notes about people who aren't dying?"

"Like you?"

"Just people who aren't clients."

I could feel him staring at the side of my face, but I couldn't bring myself to look at him.

"It says merge right to head toward Lancaster."

"Got it."

"I bet you're in a lot of people's notebooks," he said.

"Please."

"Isn't that what you want to hear?"

"Is that what you think?"

"I'm just teasing you."

"Do I look like a person who wants to be remembered?"

"I wouldn't go that far," he said.

"Just mildly narcissistic."

"Whoa, no."

I didn't mean it to sound the way it did, but it came out harsh nonetheless. My wanting him to want me had morphed into a little bit of hate. Facing down Daphne's death had made me impulsive. I had spent the morning daydreaming about all the out-of-control things I could do to annihilate my ability to feel what was coming. Everything I had thought of so far felt too involved.

17.

Daphne wanted to die at sunset, so we had to move fast. Though I was nervous, I knew enough to grab the Seconal from the trunk. I went to check on Daphne, who was sitting up comfortably in the bed that had been installed in her bedroom.

"I have the photos you wanted framed," I said. I was newly tentative around her—worried our closeness had diminished after I did not break her fall. I did not ask her about her ankle, because it didn't matter anymore.

I had framed her photos myself in cheap black Ikea frames that I had found in my closet and worried that I should have taken greater care. It's possible she would have appreciated something more gilded. I stared down at the photos of her father and mother. Her father didn't look anything like I expected—anything like mine. I noticed how she was a facsimile of her mother. Just like I was. I tried to make this mean something.

Daphne had also asked that I frame a photo of her brother. She'd never talked about him to me, but her letter to him was tender, and she called him "sweetie" over and over again. The photo was of him as a little boy, staring out a car window dreamily while holding his chin in his little fist. She said it was her favorite picture of him, one taken after a day at the beach. But to me, his dreaminess translated into a certain kind of sadness.

"I can pull in another table so they're right next to you."

"Let me see them first."

I handed them over to her, and she inspected them one at a time.

"A sweet boy," she said. "Too sensitive for this world."

She looked at me with tight rivers welling up around her lower lids.

"There's another one I want. Can you take it off the wall in the living room and bring it to me? It's the wedding picture."

"Of course."

I went to her living room and saw the tinted photo of her mother and father. Her mother was smiling and had her wedding gown swirled around her. Her father stood there proudly. Her mother's lips were painted pink, and her hair was in an updo with ringlets. They looked like movie stars, but they weren't. It was just the way people used to take pictures back then. Staring at its grandness made me realize I didn't even know where all my wedding photos were.

I pulled the heavy frame off the wall and carried it to her room. I brought a table over, near her bed, and arranged all the frames in a way I thought might please her. The wedding photo was too heavy to prop on the table. Daphne directed me by pointing and not saying a word.

I propped it against the table legs so she could see all of her family at once.

"Where's Pierre?" I asked.

"I didn't want him to remember me like this. I already said my goodbyes to him. Remember, I want to be wheeled to the window so I can see the sun go down one last time."

"Nathan's going to help me with that."

"Is the lipstick for him?"

"For you," I said. She smiled, finally warming up to me again.

"Love it. Suits you. Do you have the tube?"

"Of course."

"Will you do me up like that?"

"Sure."

I went to find my purse and saw Nathan in the kitchen, carefully opening capsules into a glass, and he looked up at me.

"She wants me to put on lipstick for her," I whispered.

"Right now?"

"That's what she wants."

He nodded and continued with what he was doing. The remaining pile of pills still seemed daunting.

"Do you remember what she wanted in her drink?" I asked.

He smiled at me and said, "Lime juice, orange juice, a hint of tequila."

"I'm not sure it was a hint."

He leaned in close, and I could feel his breath against my ear as he said, "I can wait while you make her up."

Nathan smelled like expensive body cream. Small batch, from one of those shops that doubled as meditation studios.

"I need help moving her bed to the window, though," I whispered.

He wiped his hands against his shirt and left the kitchen. I stared down at the tequila bottle, poured two fingers' worth into a glass, and downed it as quickly as I could.

I heard Daphne shout, "I want to be done up before you come in here! My hair's a mess, too."

I went into the bedroom to put on Daphne's makeup and brushed up against Nathan as he walked back to wait in the kitchen.

"Do you have any blush in there?" Daphne asked, pointing to the makeup bag I was holding. Daphne liked the idea of looking like one of those women in old movies who woke up with a full face of makeup and perfectly done lips in a Cupid's bow. It was hard to line her wrinkled mouth, but she was patient with me. The red made her skin look less gray. I took out my blush, pink, and showed it to her. There were moments when she didn't look sick at all. But even as I leaned in with my blush brush I could hear her soft wheezing.

"I look better with peachy tones," she said. I fished around in my bag but only found the pink one. She tilted her head to give me her left cheek and I applied it gently.

"Just don't make me look like one of those open-casket corpses," she said.

"I'm trying."

I let out a small, pained gasp and covered my mouth, embarrassed. I was supposed to be a professional.

"It's going to be okay," she said.

She held on to my arm as tears welled up in my eyes.

"I lived a good life. I don't need to make it to ninety-two."

"I'm so sorry," I said. "I know I'm not supposed to act like this."

"Splashing water on your face always helps."

I excused myself to go to the bathroom, even though I was afraid of the pungency of it.

This time the bathroom was clean, and the garbage empty, but the smell was still there. I ran the water and did the breathing exercises that were supposed to combat feelings of claustrophobia. A breath in, four beats, a breath out.

Nathan was knocking on the door.

"Are you okay?"

"In a minute."

I took one of Daphne's floral hand towels and dabbed my eyes. Bye, Daphne; bye, Daphne's hand towels; bye, Daphne's sunset.

When I came out of the bathroom, Nathan was already wheeling her closer to the bedroom window. We could see the whole sky from Daphne's hill.

"Better?" she asked, looking my way.

"Yes," I said, feeling guilty that I was making her death about me.

"You okay?" Nathan asked.

"I said the word 'corpse,'" Daphne said. "Sorry!"

She stared out the window, and I put my brush back into my makeup bag.

"What time is it?"

Nathan looked at his watch and said, "Ten minutes until sunset."

"That's soon," she said, somberly.

She smiled at Nathan and said, "How do I look?"

Nathan gave her a warm smile and said, "Gorgeous."

"Should we dance?" she asked.

"Whatever you want, Daphne. I'm here for you."

Daphne and I were charmed by him, as if we were in some kind of competition. But we weren't, really. In a few minutes I would be alone with him, and it made me want to burst open. We locked eyes, and I knew she wasn't going to get up. She wanted to stop playing pretend.

"Time for the cup, I guess," she said.

I went to the kitchen and took the glass full of Seconal "juice" and sniffed it.

It smelled sweet, and there were small white particles still swirling around the orange juice. The counter was covered in white dust and broken-open capsules. I had read the side effects for Seconal—anxiety, nausea, vomiting, and nightmares. I didn't want Daphne to have any of these, but I knew she wouldn't. This number of Seconal pills made you feel nothing at all. You just went to sleep and that was that. I could hear Daphne and Nathan talking, but I couldn't make out what they were saying. When I came into the bedroom, they both fell silent and looked at the cup.

"Let's see how it looks," Daphne said.

"I hope it's not too bitter for you," Nathan said.

Nathan took the glass from my hands and brought it over to Daphne's side.

"I looked up Sunrises online. You know there's a million ways to make them?"

"You should have just followed my recipe," Daphne said.

"You didn't have grenadine, though."

"You did your best. It smells right. Where's the cherry?"

"I put in two. I think they fell to the bottom," I said.

"I used to eat them by the jar," she told us. "Probably didn't help things. Formaldehyde or whatever they say."

She sniffed the contents of the glass, but didn't touch her lips to the brim.

"How do I do this?"

"Just drink it when you're ready," Nathan said.

"That's it?"

"Only if you want to," I said.

"I signed the paper."

"That doesn't mean anything," I said, nearly pleading.

They both looked at me like I had broken our unspoken contract.

"That's not the thing to say," she said, eyes narrowing at me. I wasn't allowing her to have the dignity of her own choice, and I was going to be in trouble for it. I felt embarrassed that I was thinking about myself instead of Daphne's needs.

She shook her head, looked out the window at the orange orb sliding down behind a faraway hill, and said, "Thank you for being here. It's something, isn't it?"

I didn't ask her any questions before she was gone. I didn't even try.

Nathan called the friend Daphne had delegated to find her body, while I cleaned up the kitchen and washed Daphne's glass. I walked into the bedroom and stared at her body one last time before I left. She just looked like she was sleeping, not like she was gone. I touched her face. I wanted to see her breathe, but she didn't. I pulled the blanket up to her shoulders.

I turned off her oxygen machine, and her house was finally completely still and quiet.

In the car, I put the trash bag with any remnants of our visit in the trunk. I could see Daphne's floral hand towel crammed at the bottom of my purse, far enough down to be hidden, and we set off. I got a text from Bobby saying he was going to sleep at his friend's house. It was up to me, he wrote, to make a decision about our future. I caught Nathan reading the texts, but neither of us said anything.

I pulled onto a two-lane road and parked in front of the poppy fields. Nathan was on the phone with Bethanny, letting her know that things had gone as planned. I jumped out of the parked car to the sound of Nathan asking what I was doing and raced up the hill. In the last of the dusk light, the poppies had started to twist and close against the coming night cold. I stood there in shock and bent over to catch my breath as Nathan came up behind me.

"It doesn't feel like it right now, but it's going to be okay," he said.

I turned around and—through tears—leaned in and kissed him. In the darkening poppy field, Nathan did not push me away.

"Do you want me to stop?" I asked.

"No."

"Do you have to get home?"

"No. I don't know. Do you?"

"No," I said.

"I bring my daughter here every year."

A daughter. I think he wanted me to ask him questions about her, but I wasn't about to. He didn't seem like someone's father. But he didn't say he was a husband *and* a father, and that was enough. His admission placed him in an entirely new light. He had lived a life, which was obvious, but now it had taken on new dimensions. He was responsible for someone besides himself.

"I can't go to my apartment," I said.

"There are hotels by Magic Mountain."

I assumed he had taken his daughter to the amusement park, too. Nathan and I walked down the hill toward my car, which was still running and had both doors open, as if abandoned.

Nathan looked on his phone and booked a room at the Hilton Garden Inn—the cheapest, he said. I wasn't sure if we were spending the night or just looking for a temporary bed. He gave me the option of two queens or a king bed.

"They're the same price," he said.

"Just pick one."

"You sure you want to do this?"

I moved the hand with my wedding ring away from him. I nodded yes.

He made the reservation and put his hand on my leg as we drove. I had initiated this, after all. It felt like our collective grief had merged us in some reckless way. After Daphne took her last breath, she relaxed into herself. Not a collapse, really, more like her body had stopped fighting gravity and she finally got to rest fully. I saw Nathan's eyes well up. And though I didn't ask him, I felt he didn't really want her to go, either. He'd spent less time with her than I did, but she had an effect on people. Bethanny said I would be experiencing Daphne's final moments in my dreams for weeks, months, years to come, and I was scared of that. Bethanny had shared with us her own experiences of seeing clients in her dreams. The accumulation of ghosts was inescapable, she said. Grief becomes ambient.

Nathan went to the front desk while I stayed behind in the Registration Parking lane. Families were walking through the parking lot on their way back from Magic Mountain, sunburned and cranky after a day in the sun. Was I going to have an affair in a family hotel adjacent to a theme park, in a room that promised a view of roller coasters and screaming children? In the parking lot, I didn't know. I was hungry, but there wasn't a point to bringing that up now. Something in Nathan shifted, and as he walked back to the car I could detect something like excitement. He opened the door and smiled at me.

"First floor, near the ice machine."

It occurred to me that I did this often: set something in motion and almost instantly regretted it. Though my marriage was failing, technically no one had done "the bad thing" yet. Meaning, the unforgivable act that would allow a marriage to crumble for good. Bobby and I both had our hands clean, as far as I knew. Though the beginning of our relationship was full of suspicion (mine) and denial (his), we had settled into an uneasy truce of mutual trust. Now here I was breaking that trust. It felt embarrassing and unnecessary. A friend had once told me most women waited to leave a marriage until their husbands cheated, so they had a verifiable reason to point to. It's as if they want the husbands to do it, she said, so they had an excuse to exit and force a choice that would lead to their own absolution in the matter. I wasn't looking for that kind of dramatic end.

We drove slowly through the parking lot as Nathan held a map of the premises that the woman at the counter had drawn directions onto. My whole body was buzzing—like I was about to start levitating, or maybe I was just having an anxiety attack. I tried to regulate my breathing so Nathan wouldn't notice. He pointed to a corner of the hotel and said, "It's there."

I let air seep out of my almost-closed mouth as we pulled into a spot. I turned the car off, but neither of us got out right away. I had never had sex with someone's father before. He opened the door first. I trailed him as he walked toward the room. I wanted to ask him, Don't you have any reservations about this? But his sense of urgency told me he was probably already divorced.

The room had a busy carpet, swirls that could make a person sick. He had opted for a king bed. I dropped my purse next to the TV and stood on one side of the bed while he stood on the other. We were facing off over a floral quilted divide.

"Do you think Daphne's looking down at us right now?" I asked.

"Right here?"

"Yeah, like she's floating up to heaven and looking behind her and saying, *What the hell are those two doing?*"

"I would think she'd probably be into it, knowing her."

"That does seem more likely, I guess," I said.

Someone was going to have to get on the bed first. The window drapes were open, and through the gauzy white curtains I watched the silhouettes of children jumping into the small pool right next to our room. I could hear their laughter as they splashed around and their parents yelled for them to be careful.

"Should we ask to move our room?" I asked.

"No, why?"

The splashing was loud enough so it sounded like they were swimming in the room with us.

"You're having second thoughts," he said.

"I don't know what I'm having."

He looked at me like he'd been tricked. Tricked into paying $119 for a room with a woman who had led him on. I didn't want to be that person.

"I'm going to use the bathroom," he said. "To wash my hands."

I didn't want witnesses to what we were doing, or not doing, or going to do, even. When he closed the door I thought about just taking my purse and walking right out the hotel-room door, but realized I'd likely have to face him in that fluorescent-hued conference room—or, worse, over another dying body. Or walk away from the only thing I had in my life.

I watched the shadows of children jumping past the window and got on the bed. First, I just sat on the edge, and then I moved closer to the center, shoes still on, the cheap coverlet scratching my palms. I turned to look at the rest of the bed, to see what we were working with. There were close to a dozen pillows, and I started tossing them off, one by one. I didn't care how he felt about it. I just did it. I stood up and stared at the bed, pulled the coverlet off to expose the white starched sheets, and took my things and left.

18.

I didn't make it all the way home, deciding that returning to an empty apartment would be supremely depressing. Nathan tried calling me, probably thinking I had gone for ice. His first texts didn't betray alarm, and then: *I didn't scare you off, did I?* And *Hey, this isn't funny. How am I supposed to get home?*

I drove to the beach and pulled my car alongside the Pacific Coast Highway and parked it, and even considered sleeping in the car for the night. I cracked the windows and listened to the waves crashing on the sand. It felt important for me to be by the water. We lived so far away from it, Bobby and I. Only ten miles on the map, but an hour and a half in the car.

I walked out onto the sand. It was completely silent and dark; only the lights from a nearby beach club illuminated my small patch of sand. I stared up at the sky, at the stars glittering so very far away. In front of me was the tiniest sliver of a moon—bright orange behind the black orb that obscured the rest of the bloody glow. I looked down at the collection of footprints reaching out into the darkness of the beach. I counted three stray sets among the dozens of webbed gull prints dotting the sand. I could see in the darkness that a collection of seagulls had found some space for themselves on the empty beach. They circled and swooped and walked quietly in pairs, pecking at the sand, hoping to come upon a crumb or some other leftover morsel. Some flew against the wind, suspended over me. I felt like I was on the surface of the moon, with only the sound of the ocean to ground me.

I always wished on shooting stars. As a kid I'd run outside barefoot when I knew there'd be a meteor shower. I still did. I'd make wishes on full moons and half-moons and quarter-moons. I wasn't superstitious; this kind of thing was mostly just in case.

Bobby had recently taken to telling me about other people's divorce stories. As if it was some kind of road map for ourselves, a how-to manual. Except that we'd shake our heads in sorrow for the people who were having an acrimonious time of it. Lawyer fees and custody battles—it all seemed awful to us. We were not going to be those people, he said to me once. As if he knew it was inevitable. I didn't want to go home to that inevitability, even if he wasn't there. Not just yet.

Here's what else was inevitable: your death, my death, my parents' death, your parents' death, the beginning and end of a relationship—a marriage, Bobby kept correcting me. There was a fixation on the word "marriage." It was something more intense than just a relationship. But I couldn't see the difference between the two, beyond some paperwork and a name change. Perhaps that was part of the problem. It was up to me to keep a marriage going, put in the work, and make Bobby feel as important as he thought he made me feel. But for some reason, I just couldn't do that. Nothing felt important beyond watching people die. It felt more urgent than the constraints of a marriage, of partnership, or even of building a life together. The process of dying felt inevitable, clean. But building a life together had too many variables—children, houses, sicknesses, vacations, dogs, piles of shoes, closets full of unworn clothes, broken appliances, sex, and lack of sex. Here, the only variable was the type of disease. It felt more manageable.

I had always made myself pliable to accommodate someone else's happiness, whether they asked me to or not. It was a reflex. Muscle memory from growing up in a house where only one person's happiness mattered. Except that person was never happy, and so we were left feeling disappointed in ourselves. We were never doing the right things.

I was never doing the right things. And so I settled into being disappointing early on. Here, on the beach, as I walked in the near-darkness, with only an eerie green-gray light from the faraway boardwalk, I knew I was once again a disappointment. But who would be the first to say, *I give up*? Both of us inched toward those words, but always backed away just in time. I had undoubtedly gotten closer lately. Nodding along in our therapist's office as Bobby told me he had been looking for apartments, his second venture into unknown territory in a matter of months. This admission was meant to scare, but I wasn't scared anymore. Hurt that it didn't produce the intended effect, he didn't press the point. That had been the problem all along, I was discovering. It had come to his attention that I had stopped fighting somewhere along the way, all while I thought I was keeping a secret. I knew I eventually had hundreds of nights in empty apartment bedrooms ahead of me, so tonight I wanted to sleep in my car by the side of the Pacific.

I could hear the seagulls crying through my window. I could hear the waves crashing as I stared through my windshield at the constellations I could make out. In the rearview mirror I saw a police car driving in the slow lane as an officer trained his flashlight into the windows. I turned my car on and illuminated the NO OVERNIGHT PARKING sign a few feet away. I had to go.

As I drove home from the beach and rounded my way off the 101 Freeway and through the streets of Hollywood to home, I thought about the ghosts of previous lives I had lived in L.A. hurtling past me. Apartments I had once lived in and now wanted to forget, restaurants I had gotten into fights with other boyfriends at, places where I had not been myself at all. Each time I drove through the city, I reckoned with these past versions of myself. Versions I did not like, but that had nonetheless helped me survive at the time. It felt strange to pass through these layers of myself—the ghosts who haunted me, the memories that flooded back even when I didn't want them to. This was the city I'd grown up in—not as a child, but as an adult. And I could not help flooding the city with my ghosts.

By the time I got home I was grateful Bobby wasn't there. I poured myself a drink and looked at the accumulation of our things—from swap meets and garage sales and secondhand stores in small, remote towns. Things I had haggled for, carried on my lap for long drives, things friends had admired—vintage lamps, oddities, mid-century chairs, wedding china, etc. I didn't want any of it. What did it mean that things I'd carried for decades no longer held any value to me? I had finally reached the point where I could walk away from it all.

What was next was that we would have to make a list of our things and figure out how to split them up. What did we still want to look at that would remind us of this life together? What did we buy when we were building our life together? There had been things that we did not want to move from apartment to apartment, so the culling had already begun halfway through our marriage. But what about the gifts to one another? There were things that we accepted but actually did not want or like—what was the protocol for splitting up those things? Each of us was supposed to push them onto the other person, and hold it over the other person's head that our thoughtfulness was never appreciated. It could be one last war waged to prove that we were never the right fit.

I could not imagine where to begin in our one-bedroom apartment and was glad there were no children to split. But, more pressingly, who would leave?

19.

In the weeks after Daphne's death, May Gray had settled in over Los Angeles, and it took everything I had in me to get out of bed each morning. I'd startle awake, eyes feeling like sandpaper, and stare at the endless gray looming outside my window. Even as May was winding down, I knew I would not be getting a reprieve from this feeling. June Gloom would bring more of the same overcast mornings.

What Nathan had said about not feeling like anything really mattered after doing this work echoed in my head. It felt true now. Though I had no intention of quitting Bethanny's, I called her and told her I needed some time before meeting a new client. She said she understood. She confided in me that it happened more often than not. That's why she kept the training rolling, because people were always dropping in and dropping out. She knew she was asking a lot from us and we couldn't help but be changed.

If I wasn't going to be a wife, what was I supposed to be?

I watched other women settle into the role of wife with ease. They really threw themselves into it. They *owned it.* Where were the women who felt uncomfortable in that role—or, worse, failed at being a wife altogether? The women who knew it was a job they'd never really been sure they wanted in the first place, had only taken it to follow the path of life markers set up for us. Adulthood as a stream of jobs—wife, mother, lover, caretaker.

I had suspicions that it was easier not to question these roles, as they gave us something to do—some larger purpose to strive for. Most women stayed on the path whether they liked it or not. It was simply forward momentum. Or maybe this line of thinking was precisely why I was not fit to be a wife. I didn't relish being a woman who made a winning meal or the bed just so, a woman who could juggle the inevitable tasks that weighed heavy on my side of marriage and that I was supposed to feel a sense of accomplishment from. If I left Bobby now, what was I supposed to do with my time, my life?

A man I'd met once but did not sleep with told me we are all masochists and sadists wandering around looking for our opposite. He said, "What are you, then, a masochist or a sadist?"

I had to think about it. I had, in previous relationships, tried on the role of sadist, but had not found any joy in men who played the masochist. The excitement about the power flip faded into disgust quickly.

I looked at this man and admitted I was a masochist. When I said it, I knew that he was my opposite, a sadist. I wanted him to try out the role on me, but he wouldn't, couldn't. He had already found a masochist who suited him.

But I asked him what role he played anyway, because I wanted to hear him say it.

"I'm a sadist," he told me. "You just need to find a sadist of your own."

As if it was that easy.

I was a masochist who lined up other masochists, both parties doomed from the start. Bobby and I, unaware of each other's roles, were two masochists fighting for a kind of dominance neither of us knew how to own. And as I looked around our apartment, I thought about how my default role had become sadist toward the end of our marriage—the person who performed the action that caused the most pain to the entire organism. I had turned to cruelty in hopes that Bobby would leave me, but he hung on.

"I hope you know I don't need you," I'd say from time to time, even though it felt like a lie more often than not.

"What if I need you?" he'd respond.

"It's a bad bet."

I did what I could to push him further away, but I knew I would have to be the one to cleave us in two.

When one person in a marriage is unsure who to be, both people become unmoored, losing any sense of rhythm. You have no idea how to exist around one another, much less fuck. How do you tell a person that you want to be hurt by someone else?

Bobby was waiting for me to snap out of it—to stop being crazy, even—so he could come home. If I wanted something to change I would have to be the one to do it. Though I myself had actually taken the step to go see an apartment, I could not get over the fact that he admitted he had been looking for an apartment, too. Unable to talk to each other about our mutual unmet needs, we instead idly scrolled through pictures of empty rooms in apartments available for rent.

My googling always took me back to desert homes. When we first got married, we did the thing that married couples do: we looked for a house. But we couldn't agree on anything or really afford anything, which was confusing: it felt like a natural next step after getting married. How were we to start building a life if our home still felt like a transient space? So we considered the desert, where land was cheap and we could daydream about fixing up a homesteader cabin that had good bones. We drove out to the desert and stayed in weekend rentals and looked at small homes with stairs that led to a closed-off ceiling, and homes with woodstoves, and homes with yards that had washed out during a flash flood. Back then, we stood in the middle of unincorporated dirt roads and stared at the vast expanse and smiled at each other. We could be settlers; we could really start our life together. Out there, it would be the two of us against nature. And we were excited by the prospect of working on something together. About having a plan. But, as with everything, we couldn't take action. We were trapped in indecision—each taking turns being the naysayer, or finding tiny things wrong with each house. No one had taught either of us how to be an adult who bought a house, so we floundered in our one-bedroom apartment.

Now, without any more plans, I imagined escaping to that hopeful desert feeling again. When I grew tired of looking at run-down apartments I could scarcely afford, I took to looking for houses in the desert, places to rent that were too far away for a daily drive to and from the city. The listings were full of newly renovated homes, and I thought I recognized one that Bobby and I had looked at together. Someone else was living the life we wanted.

20.

When May Gray turned into June Gloom and I could not face the relentlessness of being socked in by fog any longer, I found the courage to tell Bobby that I'd gotten an apartment of my own. The bougainvillea bloomed in magentas and purples in yards up and down our street, and the night air was thick with the smell of night-blooming flowers. Spring in Los Angeles was my favorite season, but May had been unseasonably cold, and the rain had continued well beyond what felt normal, into the first days of June. But after I said it, I drove around staring at newly blooming jacaranda trees, with their lilac petals dotting the sky and ground, and felt lighter.

What had attracted me to my new apartment was the wisteria in the front yard. When I went to look at the place, I lingered at the front window and looked at how hidden I was behind a shadow of flowers. It wouldn't feel impossible to start over here, I thought. My bank account was flush with the money I had pulled out of my retirement fund, and I finally felt I had options.

The defeat that weighed on Bobby and me was mutual, though I didn't quite want to believe that finally letting go was any kind of failure. Instead, I thought I was freeing him to be with someone who could love him the way he needed to be loved. Someone who would be the kind of wife he wanted, which was not me. It seemed impossible to say these things without appearing callous or glib, though. I just told him I was leaving, and he told me he couldn't watch me leave, and so he went away for the weekend. He could not watch me pack my things, but I had to text him periodically to ask him what I could take.

Do you want the round wooden bowl?

Leave it.

If you keep that, can I have the candlesticks?

You never used them before.

I know, but I still might, I texted back.

Are you taking the KitchenAid?

Yes, I texted him.

You never even took it out of the box during our entire marriage.

I know.

You said you would.

I can't argue about the KitchenAid again.

It'll stay in the box forever.

We never had counter space to use it.

That's not what it was, he texted back.

Then what was it?

I watched as the floating dots on the text screen undulated and then disappeared.

Leaving is logistics. It is list making; it is walking down cavernous aisles of Home Depot looking for moving boxes and packing tape; it is guilt; it is wrapping evenly split-up wedding gifts into layers and layers of clothing because you're tired of buying packing materials and you know you'll have to use the money you saved on something more urgent down the line anyway, like giving a deposit to the gas company; it is leaving the painful things behind because you cannot stand to look at them in your new life; it is knowing that you are forcing the person you are leaving to reckon with those reminders on his own; it is returning to your joint apartment days later to pick up things you forgot, only to find the picture frames you left behind that once had your wedding photos in them taken apart and lying on the floor with the pictures missing; it is realizing that you will never be touched by this person again.

It is doing the next action until all the actions accumulate into your being on your own in a new place and feeling free and feeling loss. Leaving is the initial rush of having your own space and your own time and your own life, but with an absence that feels so vast that it is literally unquantifiable. It is being afraid to keep the windows open at night because you no longer have someone to protect you, and so you sleep in two-hour increments, which you have convinced yourself will make you feel safer in your new life, this life you chose, this life without your partner. It is the life you chose but a choice you do not know how to talk about yet. It has been a long time coming and you have prepared yourself for it for months, and so you are not the surprised person in this scenario—you are the person who had the plan all along. But when people see you they act like someone has died, and they turn away from you, because they don't know how to talk about divorce unless they've gone through it themselves.

These are the things I felt about the end of my marriage, which seemed like it had come quickly and not quickly enough at all. It had only taken a few weeks between the time I told Bobby that I was leaving and sleeping in a new apartment on the sofa we had bought together. New furniture comes in waves, but I had packed and unpacked my moving boxes in the span of a weekend. I was that eager to destroy the evidence of my decision—to make it seem as if I had been in my new apartment all this time and a dislocation had not occurred. There is something to be said about being the person who gets to move on in a new place—to start fresh, as people like to say. Meanwhile, the person who has chosen to stay behind is trapped among remnants of a familiar and distant life as they try to piece together a new way of being in an apartment that was once inhabited by someone they loved, or maybe even still love.

But the person who hurt them might have left behind a toothbrush, or, worse yet, a small collection of hair loosely bundled in a corner that wouldn't be discovered until weeks later. This small, tumbleweed-like tuft is particularly painful because it is both an intimate part of a loved one and a reminder of a previous life. I tried to be dutiful in not leaving behind parts of myself, of my body, but there are always strays.

ONE OF THE FIRST NIGHTS I slept in my new apartment, I dreamed of being in a hospital waiting room. There were other women in there with me, pregnant and not, and we were waiting for our names to be called. Thumbing through issues of *People* and *Us Weekly* as we waited. The phone kept ringing. Two women in pink scrubs wheeled a gong out to the waiting room. I was trapped in Daphne's cancer ward, but no one seemed to be sick. These women were happy—blonde, brunette, a sea of white women on high alert. They all seemed to know why we were here.

The first nurse looked at her chart and said, "Hillary Johnson?" Hillary, a twentysomething in a striped boatneck shirt, blue capris, and a headband, jumped up and threw down her magazine. She was ready to win a game show. She was ready to hit the gong.

"Five years!" the nurses cooed.

Hillary clapped her hands and said, "It's true!"

"That's the wood anniversary," one of the nurses said.

Another nurse looked at her and said, "I'm still on paper."

"You'll make it," Hillary said. "You'll all make it."

The women around me clapped and looked on with envy. The woman next to me, who was dressed in a black sheath suitable for an interview, leaned in and whispered, "I'm a newlywed."

"Congratulations," I said, really focused on meaning it.

"Come up here and claim your reward," the nurses said.

Hillary ran to the gong and pulled the mallet from the nurse's hand.

"I've never done this before," she said.

"Hit it like you mean it," the nurse said.

"I'm six weeks along," she said.

"It won't hurt the baby to celebrate your achievement," the nurse said, hand on her shoulder.

"More to celebrate," the other nurse added.

Hillary slammed the mallet into the gong so hard that it nearly knocked her backward.

"I could feel it in my teeth," she said. "I hope my baby couldn't feel the jolt."

"It can't feel anything," I said.

I woke up with a start, my heart racing. I didn't want to be the kind of person who didn't want others to make it.

21.

When you are alone, there is suddenly so much more time to fill. In my first month alone, I looked for ways to structure my time while trying to avoid people—friends, or anyone—who would potentially ask me how Bobby was doing. I let Bobby stick to the meet-and-greets, knowing it meant that he would probably win most of our friends in the divorce. That's what happens when you get to lead how the story gets told. My absence—and silence—meant that I was probably hiding something.

Or that I had some sense of shame about it. I only felt ashamed at feeling liberated for the first time in a long time. I had left behind persistent despair. But no one says a sense of liberation is an okay feeling to have when you leave a marriage. I thought about how it would look to take vacation photos, alone or with friends, looking visibly happy, and how people would react to not seeing me laid out on the floor. Or if people would judge me for not being destroyed by my choice. I wondered how long I was supposed to perform some kind of grief to adequately convey to others how much I cared about my marriage. More important, why did I have to carry other people's feelings about the end of my marriage?

I had cared about my marriage *and* I felt a sense of relief.

Not wanting to carry the burden of other people's feelings about what I had done naturally made me feel like a piece of shit. I had made a choice that caused an unwelcome shift in the lives of those around us, people who were expecting grandchildren, or at least well-rounded family get-togethers.

What was interesting is that women I only knew in the most minor way started e-mailing me asking for drink dates, and confiding in their e-mails that they, too, were unhappy in their marriages. They wanted to feel out if leaving was worth it, so they wanted to get together and discuss what being single was like.

Before I understood what they were asking, I took a friend up on one of these drinks dates. I chose somewhere nearby, so I could walk there, and when I arrived she was already sitting at the bar with a glass of wine. As I sat down next to her she told me how good I looked and stared at me, looking for any betrayal of how I was actually doing. I was spending more time on a beauty routine for my face, poking and prodding at my pores, hairs that had begun to sprout on my chin and other parts, which had seemed horrifying to consider just a decade before. She told me my maintenance routine was working.

"So how is it?"

"All of it or . . . ?" I asked.

"Being alone."

"It's hard, but I don't remember the last time I had this much time to focus on what I want."

"What a dream," she said.

She was blond like me, but much slimmer, from years of personal training sessions three times a week. Her hair was the kind that could hold a style with little effort and always looked freshly dyed. She was a person you would see on the street and instantly envy. Sometimes I felt like she wanted to be friends so she could always know where she was in the hierarchy of life. And here she was confiding in me about her general unhappiness. She wasn't at the point of doing something irreversible, but a kind of malaise had settled over her life.

"I think my husband has a girlfriend stashed somewhere."

"You do?"

"Not really, actually. It just sounds better than admitting that we're both bored with each other."

"It's the boredom that gets you."

"Everything is so tedious. We even have to make sure to schedule sex, because that's become tedious, too."

"Is the schedule working?" I asked.

"I feel like I could be having a lot more sex if I wasn't married. How do you keep the excitement going? Does anyone know?"

"I don't."

She turned to me, and I knew what she was going to ask, because she leaned in closer to me and she had just ordered her third glass of wine.

"You must see so many different dicks now."

I knew I was to perform the role of single friend she could live vicariously through. I could be honest and say I had been avoiding men altogether, which would make it seem like being alone was living at a deficit, or I could lie and let her have her fantasy of a different kind of life that felt more thrilling.

I knew these were the roles, because I had, at one point, asked single friends to play them for me, too. These conversations were to see how it was "out there."

"It's gotten so boring that I appreciate that Todd bends me

over, so we don't have to look at each other when we fuck, so I can fantasize about someone else in peace."

"You could just close your eyes," I said.

"He complains when I do that. He asks where I am. I want to tell him, I'm spread out underneath you, but I know you're just thinking about some online cam girl."

"Better than someone in real life, no?"

I let her continue while I smiled at the bartender, whom I had become friendly with since moving to the neighborhood, and worried he was judging me for this conversation. She was getting louder and talking more animatedly about dicks, but happy hour wasn't over. I hoped she hadn't driven herself here.

I capped myself at four glasses of wine, which she paid for. After we hugged, I walked home, one foot in front of the other, and told myself I should avoid probing e-mails from now on. She would not leave her husband, because I had not made a compelling case for giving up all the accessories to her life, and all the forward momentum that came with being a married couple. She did not pity me, but she did not envy me strongly enough, either. She said she would probably be getting pregnant soon, and I knew I'd never see her again after that.

Instead of going out on more of these humiliating meet-ups, I focused on the following: online shopping for housewares, most of which never left my shopping cart; spending more time at the wine store and developing crushes on the wine-store employees, who I believed were emotionally invested in my having a good time; telling myself I had to leave my apartment at least once a day, and then doing so—either to take a walk for a minimum of forty-five minutes to breathe fresh air and look at the sky, or to go to Ralphs, where I would wander the aisles staring at food I no longer had any appetite for. I filled my refrigerator full of food that would inevitably need to be thrown away a week or two later, while wondering how many times was too many times to go to the wine store. I had taken to going once a week to collect an assortment of under-ten-dollar bottles of wine to bring home, usually capped at six. I was too embarrassed to make an unfortunate second trip later in the week, when my empty bottles filled the trash. I also worried what would happen when my weed pen ran out. Bobby had bought me one with 250 hits in it and I had lost count of how many I had actually taken. I worried every hit would be my last, and I couldn't afford to get another. I started a complicated system for rationing all my substances.

I also logged in to my account each morning to see all the money I had pulled out of my 401(k). The apartment wasn't inexpensive, and the first month plus security deposit had made a dent. I knew I had to go back to Bethanny.

She called me one afternoon to say that she had a check waiting for me—from my work with Daphne. She said she could mail it if I wanted to give her my address but she'd love it if I came to the sessions she was having so we could chat. I told her Bobby and I had separated. She said big life changes like this weren't uncommon because what we did was clarifying. She ended the call with "We are here when you're ready to come back."

I was tired of just drinking and getting high. I was also spending too much time looking at strangers' grief blogs. I knew I was a helper, not just someone sleepwalking through life anymore. On some death blogs there was a focus on final breaths, how they were so important and meaningful. But I knew they weren't. Daphne was gone well before she exhaled her final breath. I touched her as her breath became raspy and her hands were already starting to feel cold. Consciousness had already left her, I could tell.

Bethanny said there was such a fetish around final breaths, but the person was already gone by then and their spirit had gone with them. The body was doing something natural by expelling air, and when we waited for it—focused on it—we missed the real final moments that indicated the end. It was like people's fixation with the final fight of a marriage: the end had come long before that final fissure, yet people always wanted to know what the breaking point was.

Still, I didn't wade in and say anything on the comment boards. People got really touchy about that stuff. Also, I wasn't going to be judgmental about what people wanted to hold on to. The only thing I cared about was not letting people die alone. I read stories on the boards about family members who weren't found for days, the kind of guilt that comes with not having checked in for a while, the kinds of things that happen to a body in that time. I was worried that would be me one day.

Without Bobby as an anchor to "the real world," my preoccupation with death ballooned. I watched YouTube videos of other people involved in final exits, testimonials from patients in Switzerland before they passed. Nathan had called me twice, and though it felt nice to know someone cared about where I was, I couldn't bring myself to call him back. Maybe Bethanny had told him I was going through something.

How could I prepare myself to come back and not feel anything for the people I was helping? I felt like I was trying to crack some code of how to become desensitized—feel less. Bethanny would always say it was important to feel the full spectrum of feelings, but I didn't think so.

I also mostly avoided calls from my parents, because they were deeply invested in the moving-on portion of the divorce and needed frequent progress reports. I wanted to ask them for money but couldn't bring myself to do it. If they thought I was struggling they would start to worry, and they had enough to worry about.

Anything I would say about my current state of mind would upset them.

The times I had answered, my mother would break into our conversations with "Are you happy?"

To which I would answer, "Of course not."

"Why not?"

"Mom, stop."

"I want you to meet someone nice."

Everyone wanted me to meet someone nice. Everyone wanted me to meet someone. In the middle of July, just as the city had started to heat up, a friend who didn't know Bobby invited me to a dinner party. I scanned the invite list and noticed it was all couples. I was starting my life as a single person floating through couple parties. I decided to go see what it would feel like. What no one tells you is that a single woman at a dinner party is, more often than not, seen as a threat.

The house reminded me of what I did not have—might never have—in the form of a California Craftsman in Echo Park with a cute front lawn punctuated with bougainvillea and walls of jasmine. Inside, the house had a few kids' toys strewn about tasteful, lived-in furniture. The couples were already milling around and talking to each other like they had known one another for years, and lived close enough so their children could go to school together. They were my age, but appeared to have done all the right things. I placed the bottle I was holding among the other bottles that had amassed on the table and went into the backyard, which, though similar to other backyards in similar houses crawling up and down the Eastside hills of Los Angeles, was also a touch more serene. There was an effortlessness about the lights strung around the frame of a pagoda where other couples, in the cute outfits that creative couples in L.A. wear (sack dresses, Hasbeens clogs), were talking in pairs. I took a breath and walked into the mix and poured myself a glass of wine.

I went through the motions of asking, "How do you know the host?" while I looked for the host. She was a friend from a previous job who sent me yearly invites to garden parties that I never attended. Every year a freshly designed envelope would show up in my e-mail inbox, inviting me and Bobby. I didn't like couple things: couple dinners, couple vacations, and movie outings with couple dinner conversations afterward.

I listened as people talked about buying houses, or looking to have another child, and felt like a foreigner in this strange land where everyone had their shit together. I went to sit at a picnic table that had been set up and did breathing exercises while I stared at a vine of jasmine that a gardener had purposely draped over a fence separating this house from the house next door, which was nearly identical.

"How do you know the host?"

I turned around and saw a man staring at me with a smile. He had salt-and-pepper hair that looked like it had appeared on his head a decade too soon. And the cuffs of his button-down shirt looked like they had taken him more than a few minutes to roll to an adequately effortless length, which could convey "laid-back."

"I don't remember, actually."

My chest seized for a moment. Was this a person who was hitting on me or just a person? I looked at his fingers and saw a ring and let go of my breath. I was safe—he was off-limits.

"Mysterious."

"A meet-up for women, I think."

"Power women."

"Women without power."

"Even better," he said.

"You think so?"

It was at this point that his wife walked over to present herself as "the wife," so there would be no question of supremacy.

Already a little drunk, she eyed me as she asked my name.

"I like when young women are named old-women names," she said.

"Sarah," her husband said.

"It's a compliment."

"I didn't say 'Esther.'"

"'Evelyn' counts, too," she said.

He smiled at me, a "bear with us" smile.

She was holding someone's phone and shoved it into her husband's face.

"Look at Peggy's vacation photos."

She was done sizing me up. I could tell we weren't that far apart in age, but she had the look of someone who was the boss at her job, and her husband had the look of someone who had been slightly emasculated over the course of the last decade.

"Let me go find her so she can tell us where she went."

She disappeared into the couples. I adjusted my leg, which was falling asleep, and said, "I need to move my leg, but I don't want to kick you."

"You can kick me, but I'll want to pay you for it."

He smiled at me. It was a secret moment he wanted to share with me. A cue that he was down with having fun. I did not find it sexy. Instead, I wondered if Bobby had ever said that to another woman when we were married.

"Here she is," his wife said. She stumbled over with another woman, and I got up to make room for them. They didn't want me looking at their vacation photos.

I walked across the lawn and saw the host, my friend, cooking in the kitchen through the back window. I avoided the window and walked down the side of the house that led to the driveway and onto the street. The house was warmly lit and filled with friends, couples searching for sameness. I walked down the street, breathing in the cool night air, and looked for my car.

22.

There was a time when I could get prescriptions for Xanax and Klonopin that could last me several months—ninety pills at a time, even—but the opioid epidemic made doctors taper off their lavish prescription and refill policies. At least that's what I told myself about why Dr. Kassell suddenly was cutting me off at thirty pills max, with a visit necessary for any kind of refill so we could "talk." Bobby had been kind enough to keep me on his insurance through the rest of the year, and I felt I needed to take better care of myself, because after that I was on my own. I scheduled a physical, but my main concern was making sure I could sleep through the night. I didn't have cable anymore, so I spent my nights wandering my apartment looking for things to clean. It was an immaculate space no one ever came to see.

In Dr. Kassell's office, I stared at the pictures on her wall of far-flung places that she liked to hike through. The big mountains that kill people from time to time. She had mastered them all and wanted patients to see evidence of her healthy living. I gave her my ready spiel about getting a divorce and maybe being depressed but mostly being anxious. Dr. Kassell asked, "But don't you feel free?"

"Mostly, yes."

"You don't have kids, right?"

"Definitely not."

"You're lucky."

"Why?"

"I stayed an extra ten years because of my kids." She wrote some notes down on her chart and said, "It'll get better."

"I'm not unhappy," I said. "I'm just scared of the noises outside my window at night."

"You'll get used to it," she said.

"It sounds like snarling."

"It's L.A. I'm sure it's a coyote or something."

I didn't expect the city to feel so feral when I was alone, but Dr. Kassell was right—L.A. was wild. And I felt like I was in the wildest part of it. On a hill, where there was room for animals to congregate and grow into packs. A place where possums raced by my screen door and whole families of raccoons stood on my doorstep, staring at me, as if they wanted to join me on the sofa. At night, when sirens rushed by, coyotes joined together in howling song, vibrating long after the ambulances were gone. This is what I loved about the city and this is what I feared as I went through it alone.

"I'm on the ground floor again," I said. Not wanting to spell out what I was trying to spell out about living alone as a woman—rape, murder, everything you see on true-crime shows that felt applicable only to women.

I could see she was tapping in a prescription for Xanax, capping it once again at thirty.

"Could I have more?" I asked.

"Have you seen a therapist?" she asked.

I had seen many over the years. Warm auntlike women who wore shawls. Clinical women in hospital coats. My favorite was a middle-aged man I liked to act out father-daughter scenarios with—he would tell me how proud he was of me and then angrily cry that my life had value when I told him I didn't care what happened to me in certain situations. I had moved away from him to be with Bobby and thought about him at least once a week. I wanted to know if he missed me and thought about me as much as I thought about him. I didn't want to fill my life up with more office visits. I could hardly bring myself to drive to see Dr. Kassell for my pill refills.

She said, "Have you tried meditation?"

She wrote down a woman's name and number and passed it to me. I smiled and took the paper and stopped in the bathroom before leaving the office.

There, I spotted a jar of condoms in their "grab what you like" cabinet. I did. I took several handfuls, as if willing some sex into existence. As if there was a newfound urgency to being with someone else. There was not.

While I waited for my prescription to be filled, I went to sit in the bar of the Beverly Wilshire Hotel. There were Lamborghinis, Ferraris, Bugattis, tourists lining the driveway, and I felt like someone important weaving through them all. Tour guides were shuttling out-of-towners past the hotel, urging them to take pictures of the "hotel from *Pretty Woman*." And they did, taking pictures of the hotel sign while excitedly whispering that this was probably their favorite moment of the entire Beverly Hills experience.

Inside, I took a seat at the bar, noticing that we were well past the afternoon lunch crowd. I ordered a glass of Sauvignon Blanc, and then another, and tried to determine if I should forgo having dinner so I could afford a third. I had taken to using my credit card too liberally and knew I had to cut it out.

A man in khaki shorts and a golf shirt sat down two seats away from me, and I could tell he was already drunk. He ordered a Negroni and assessed the situation—me. Even though I did not look up, I noticed him scan the bar to see if there was anything better, but it was just the two of us, trying to wash away the day. I wondered if I looked like a woman who had two dozen free condoms stuffed at the bottom of her purse, or just like a moderately well-dressed woman, alone at a bar in the latter half of an afternoon, drinking alone.

He made a joke and I politely smiled; perhaps I even laughed. He knew then that he had an in. He leaned over and said his name was Roger, and I could feel his eagerness for connection. He was balding, and he looked at me, trying to gauge my age, and said he was forty-four. He waved his hand dismissively, knowing it was rude of him to ask my age.

There was a moment somewhere between leaving Nathan in the hotel room and leaving Bobby for good when I had decided that the things I had done had made me a sponge for people who needed to over-share.

"I'm Evelyn," I said, and smiled. We once again assessed each other, he deciding I was someone he could have sex with, and I deciding he was someone I could not. The bartender looked nervous on my behalf.

Roger said, "I own horses."

He was starting out bold, and I appreciated it.

"I don't think I've ever met anyone who owns horses," I said.

"My friends own sports teams."

"How do you feel about that?" I said, sensing it was a pain point for him.

"They want the best for me," Roger said.

"Who doesn't?"

We were getting into our groove now.

"I don't want anything from you," he said. "I just want to talk."

"I bet a lot of people want something from you, though."

"Don't you know it."

It was my sense, and not from experience, that it was hard being rich sometimes, that someone always had an angle to work on you. I conveyed a sense of compassion for the uncomfortable bind Roger must have found himself in often—being voraciously needed—so he could know I didn't want anything from him.

"I'm here for a memorial. My mother. She loved horses, too."

"I'm sorry, Roger," I said.

"She died last year, but I couldn't face a memorial for her until now. Everyone was nice about it."

"Grief takes time," I said. "It's best not to avoid it."

He swiveled to face me and ordered another Negroni.

"I have a few girlfriends around," he said.

"I'm sure they're helping. I bet they like your horses, too."

"I'm a successful person."

"I can tell."

"But I quit my job right after my mother died. It was a new job. I can sell anything to anyone, but I didn't care anymore."

"I bet you made everyone your bitch," I said.

I really don't know why I said that, except that it seemed like something top sales guys said to each other to rile each other up. He flinched and then nodded.

"I did, I guess."

He paused and then changed the subject.

"My friends, my friends did a sort of intervention for me this week. Because . . . it's not that I wanted to die or anything. I'm successful, so I have things. But it's tough. I think about her every day."

He was leaning in closer and so was I.

"Do you dream about her?"

"Three times so far," he said. "But the dream always ends too quick. I want to see her for longer."

"She's telling you she's okay."

"Do you think so?"

"I bet people don't understand what you understand now," I said.

"My girlfriends don't understand. One was a housewife on a reality show."

"I love that show," I said.

"Do you want to see a picture?"

He scrolled through his phone and I stared at his life, pictures of boats and beaches, and he finally settled on a photo of a woman in a bikini wearing sunglasses and a hat and showed it to me proudly.

"I can only see her boobs, but I think I recognize them," I said.

He looked at me and winked.

"I didn't pay for them, though," he said. "I already paid for my ex-wife's boobs." He then looked down at mine in some kind of reflex, and silently nodded in appreciation.

We were strange companions, but companions for the afternoon nonetheless. I would never see Roger again, but I wanted to handle his grief, make him feel less alone, and position myself as the type of woman who could.

"I have to go, Roger."

He was not accustomed to having people leave him, I could tell. He got up to hug me, and it felt nice to be touched. I realized just then that I had not been touched since Nathan in the poppy field, months before. How was that possible? Overcome, I whispered, "It's hard now but you will get through it, I promise. Just hang in there."

When I pulled away from him he held my arms out so he could look at me fully, sliding his eyes up and down to size up my body. In that moment, he became just a drunk, successful man again, rather than a person leveled by grief. He nodded and smiled at me, shook his head in appreciation. I was wanted. I had passed some kind of test.

On the drive home, I thought about Bobby trying to meet women in bars. How he'd do it, if he'd succeed or not—what strategies and tactics he'd employ. I wanted him to win—to regain his masculinity and to feel wanted by someone again. It was strange for me not to feel any hostility toward him. I had spent much of our relationship cataloguing grievances and resentments, employing them as needed during arguments like dozens of small poison darts. I liked to catch him off guard, especially when things were going well. A nice dinner, a nice walk. I was expert at wrecking them. We had been trapped, one of those couples who sat in uncomfortable silence across wooden tables at low-lit restaurants. The kind that we shared horrified glances about when we first got together, silently assuring one another that we'd never end up like that. The progression was gradual, though.

When we were married I used to stay up late worried that Bobby would meet someone else. I did not become a person who checked his phone or his computer until a few years in.

Nothing out of the ordinary was happening. Nothing I wasn't doing myself.

BOBBY TEXTED ME to invite me over to his apartment—our old apartment—to catch up one evening. I knew it was an innocuous invitation. We had remained something like friends, texting each other every so often, him mostly, to give updates. Trips, friends we had heard from and those we had not.

I drove past our old apartment frequently. It did not hurt. Once, I had begged a friend to drive me past an ex-lover's house, and we sat there for fifteen minutes while I searched for how to feel, looking for a weight that was not there. Why had I always been trying to inflict meaning on people, places, and things? They didn't need to hurt. But maybe I couldn't allow myself to feel anything besides pain. Everything else—happiness, contentment—felt unsafe.

When I got to Bobby's, I walked up assuredly, like I still lived there. I saw old neighbors who had watched me walk out with my boxes. We smiled at each other like nothing had happened. Like I was coming home from work again. Like I hadn't been missing for weeks.

Inside, Bobby had mixed the things I had left behind with new items that gave the place a more masculine feel. It was like a house that belonged to someone who had eclectic taste, but my taste was still there, my touches, my years of collecting—things I had left behind so as not to look selfish. It was no doubt impressive to women who came over now. My collection of vintage lamps and trinkets gave the appearance of a single man who had his shit together.

While we talked, caught up on each other's lives, in a

conversation that featured no small slights, no sense of resentment, his phone buzzed. He looked down at it and smiled. It was intimate in a way that made me feel embarrassed. Like I was watching the start of something, like I was intruding on someone else's beginning.

"I'm sorry," Bobby said.

"It's fine," I said.

But he went back to looking at his phone and texting.

I thought about one of our first dates, after we had just slept together for the first time. His phone had buzzed then, too. We were at a restaurant, about to go to a party where I would meet his friends for the first time. People whom I did not know, but who had seen him bring women around before.

"Who is that?" I had asked in the restaurant years ago.

Bobby looked up, still smiling, caught in the moment.

"A friend. It's nothing. She's . . ."

I don't think I heard anything else.

"Does she know you're out with someone else?"

"I met her before you," he said.

"Does she know about me?"

"No, not really."

His smile faded. He didn't realize what war he was in. Instead of saying more, I sat in silence. I could have, and should have, left then. We were at the start of our relationship and already these insertions of other people into our twosome were haunting us. Or, more specifically, haunting me. It was in that moment that I catalogued my first resentment, yet still vowed to stay. I wanted to win.

I didn't tell him that this moment of joy that had nothing to do with me, but was nonetheless unfolding in front of me, hurt.

And I wondered why I kept confusing people—him and everyone who came before him—about how to treat me.

As I watched him rush to answer a new text with a smile, as if I wasn't even there, I was hurt again. He was trying to maintain a beginning with someone else. I didn't leave him back then in the restaurant, when it would hardly have hurt to leave, because I wanted him to choose me.

But, sitting there, in the apartment we had inhabited together for a number of years, I watched that intimate moment of joy, and knew there was nothing left to win.

I looked at his fingers typing and noticed he was no longer wearing his wedding ring. I looked down at mine, still there, and felt foolish in front of him.

23.

I finally called Bethanny toward the end of July, not long after my encounter with Bobby. She told me to come to a Saturday session.

"As a refresher," she said.

When I did, I parked on the street so I wouldn't have to smile and nod at anyone in the parking lot. I watched people who had not been in my training group mingle with each other. I didn't know how far along they were, but I saw they had already gotten the packets that held their own end-of-life directives. I made sure to pick a row no one else was sitting in so I didn't need to interact with anyone. I wasn't quite like Lorraine or Nathan, but I had been out in the field already, so I knew more than these trainees did. I did not have their same vibrant excitement about being "helpers." I felt a hand on my shoulder and turned to see Bethanny standing there. Reactively, I got up and let her embrace me.

"It's so good to see you," she said. "I have your check. Hold on."

She went to her purse and brought me back an envelope.

"Thanks," I said.

"I can sense you've been having a hard time, but it's part of the process."

"It is?"

"A rabbi once told me that we all live with a certain cognitive dissonance as we navigate the challenges of this world. We struggle with a duality that's rooted in the foundation of our existence. We are drawn between the realness of the body—the mundane, if you want to call it that—and the soul, which is the divine. The challenge and hope in our lives is to unite the two in order to bring about transcendence. In death, we are finally freed from the limitations of the mundane."

She smiled at me benevolently.

"That's what we're helping people do. But we're left behind with all these confusing and painful feelings—until it's our turn to go and be free," she continued.

"All right," I said. "That makes sense."

"Good."

Someone else tapped her on the shoulder and she said, "We can talk more after."

She wafted toward the front of the room. Because she wore dresses that reached the floor, it felt like she was hovering above it. She started on her speech about pain-avoidance techniques, and I watched people try to determine their own pain levels as they asked each other "How do you avoid pain?"

I was again among people finding a certain kind of transcendence while I struggled with even having a sense of self. I looked down at my lap and saw the envelope sitting there. I opened it and saw the check was made out for seven hundred dollars. Though I was grateful for the sum, I had mixed feelings about what it meant for her to standardize this kind of thing. I watched each person having an epiphany. We were hardly the first set of people in Los Angeles to pay money to learn how to feel. But I wanted to tell them that Bethanny wasn't exactly setting them free here.

At the end of the exercise, they were as awe-inspired as our group had been, and I watched all of them embrace in some kind of pact of the forever-changed. I wanted to feel that. I really did. I hung back until the last of the devoted had fawned over Bethanny. When I finally reached her, the conference room had thinned out.

"I'm ready to come back," I said.

"I'm so glad," she said, and smiled at me. "I have a client for you. Lawrence has a lot of personality, and he'll be ready to meet you soon. I've done a lot of the initial work. Do you want to meet with him alone, or would you like me to be with you?"

"How far have you gotten?" I asked.

"We've worked our way through pain avoidance, a few of his letters, and really it's just a matter of getting through the final questions of his questionnaire."

"I can do that," I said.

"I want to ease you back in."

"What method does he prefer?"

"He is adamant about a hood, but I'm going to handle that. I just want you to focus on finishing up the questions. The rate will be the same. He just really needs some companionship."

The next morning, I woke up to my phone ringing and realized I had forgotten to put it on Silent. I didn't know what time it was or who would be calling me. The list had gotten short since I had stopped responding to most everyone's texts. I didn't recognize the number and hesitated picking up, but the ringing felt like an emergency.

"Hello?"

"Is this Evelyn?"

She said she was a friend of Daphne's. Daphne had told her she could use me as a backup for Pierre.

"It's not that I don't want Pierre," she said. "He's just a handful."

"He seemed pretty relaxed when I was with him."

"She said he really liked you."

"Do you need something?"

"Maybe just a little break."

I agreed to take Pierre for a few days, perhaps because I was more pliant in my half-asleep, 1.5-milligrams-of-Xanax state. I repeated "just a few days" four or five times to be sure. Even though I didn't have any plans and I lived in walking distance to a dog park, the responsibility of caring for Pierre felt immense.

The woman dropped him off and gave me a roll of dog-waste bags, Pierre's sleeping pad, and a bag of food. She told me I could use my own bowls, because she had forgotten them.

She looked up and down my street and said, "Pierre will have a lot to sniff here."

I had a terrible feeling I would never see her again, but she assured me she'd be back soon. She just had to see her children for a few days and could not manage both. I looked at her and wondered how close she'd been to Daphne—if I could trade taking care of Pierre for more information about her.

"He's been a nice reminder of her. Sometimes I put my face in his fur and cry."

I looked down at Pierre and held his leash. He sniffed around my stoop and lifted his leg to mark it as she disappeared back in her car and drove off.

I took Pierre to my apartment and let him off his leash. He ran from room to room, sniffing, and I worried he might pee somewhere, or worse. I hovered over him as he checked things out.

"Pierre, relax."

He ignored me and kept pacing. I looked at my bowls, new on clearance from Crate & Barrel, ones I had never used before because I hadn't had anyone over yet, and filled them with water and kibble and put them on the floor. He just looked at me, upset.

"Do you need to go out?"

He lay down on his side and opened his legs, his erection blooming. I felt bad for him all of a sudden, his vulnerabilities always on display.

"Relax a little, Pierre."

He jumped up again and came toward me. I petted his head and said, "Just calm down."

I couldn't take him to the dog park like that. The other dogs would harass him.

Instead, I took Pierre on a long walk. He seemed to calm down later in the evening. I put his bed near mine, and he curled into it and went to sleep. Listening to him breathe and groan in his sleep, I thought of Daphne. I wondered if she could see us. Me and Pierre, together again. I watched him snore until I fell asleep, too. I didn't wake up once in the night.

WHEN I WOKE UP in the morning, I felt as if Daphne had given me a test posthumously and I had passed it. I was a responsible person. I looked down at Pierre and he was still sleeping.

"You're a good boy," I whispered.

He looked up at me and whimpered.

"Do you need to go out?"

He whimpered again.

I got out of bed and he struggled to get up, but couldn't.

"What's wrong?"

He looked up at me and acted like he was stuck on the bed.

As panic started to set in, I asked him again what was wrong, as if expecting some kind of answer.

He put his head down, depressed.

I leaned down and petted him and asked him if he was sick.

"Fuck, don't do this to me, Pierre."

I gently pulled at his paw and he whimpered. I apologized and stared at him. He tried to get up again but couldn't.

I googled "paralyzed dog" and everything alarming came up in return.

I had to call Daphne's friend to tell her what was happening. Maybe Pierre had done this before. She didn't answer. I tried again. Finally, I left a helpless message on her voice mail while I stared at Pierre's drooping head.

I called the animal hospital, and they told me to bring him in. I had no idea how much it would cost or how I would carry Pierre to my car.

I tried to coax Pierre up again, and tried to move my hands under his belly to help him up as he whimpered. He looked at me with his sad eyes, immobile.

I ran around my bedroom putting clothes on as Pierre watched me. I even brought his food bowl into the bedroom, hoping that would rouse him. It didn't.

"What did I do?" I whispered at him. "Did we walk too much yesterday?" I thought about how I had made him run a little and felt awash with guilt.

I got on all fours and tried to talk to him, reason with him.

"I can help you, but you need to work with me."

I decided I would carry both him and his bed as one. First, I ran down to my car and unlocked it, then ran back to my house and gently picked up Pierre's bed. He was heavier than he looked. We struggled to the car, him whimpering and me huffing. As I tried to set him in the back seat, I was near tears, thinking I had irreversibly harmed Daphne's dog. I ran back and locked up my house and drove him to the hospital, checking the rearview mirror as he stared back at me.

"We're going to fix this," I said. "We're going to figure this out."

At the hospital, I went to the back seat, opened the door, and put on Pierre's leash. He pushed past me and jumped onto the ground. We stared at each other briefly, and then he lifted his leg and peed on my tire.

"What the fuck," I said. He looked at me with casual indifference.

I slowly walked him inside, confused and getting a little bit pissed. There was another dog in there, a mutt, and Pierre tried to pull toward him.

"I called about the paralyzed dog," I said to the nurse at the counter.

We both looked down at Pierre just standing there.

"I don't know why he's better now."

She smiled at me like she had seen this before—maybe all the time, even. She told me it happens, but I was too shocked to ask when. I just stared down at Pierre, who let out a little wag.

"Do you want to see the doctor still?"

"What if it happens again?"

"We won't know what's wrong with him unless we look at him."

"We're here," I said.

She gave me forms to fill out, and Pierre ambled beside me as I sat down.

"What are you doing?" I asked him, and he just stared back at me.

"Evelyn?"

The doctor was balding and seemed nice enough. As we walked to a back room, I tried to explain that Pierre had just started walking again. That Daphne was dead. That I was an emergency contact ill-equipped to handle emergencies.

All he said in response was "Will you put him on the table?"

I picked the dog up and put him on the table, and the doctor looked at each paw.

"Did he step on something?"

"I don't think so."

"Which leg was in distress?"

"All of them. Or maybe just the back ones. I don't know."

"Was he dragging his paws at all?"

"I only just got him yesterday."

"Right."

He kept checking Pierre. His erection bloomed, and I was embarrassed for both of us.

"Not now," I said.

"I can't tell anything without an X-ray or an MRI. But it doesn't seem like he has anything wrong with him."

"I don't think I can afford tests."

"We might just have to express his anal glands. Sometimes that has an effect on them. Do you want to be in here for that?"

"No," I said, shaking my head. "I really don't."

"I can get a nurse to hold him."

Pierre peered at me. I turned and left the room anyway.

The doctor came out with Pierre and a bottle of pills.

"Painkillers," he said. "In case his soreness comes back. Call if you need a refill."

I took the bottle of pills from him, paid the bill of $120 with my credit card, and walked Pierre back to the car.

At home, I broke the pill apart like the doctor had told me and gave half to Pierre with a treat. He walked around the house like normal for a few minutes, and then wandered over to his bed before passing out.

I stared at the pill bottle—the dosage, Pierre's name, my address. The label said NOT FOR HUMAN CONSUMPTION. I wondered why. What could be so different about treating a dog's pain and a human's? The pills were white and oblong, like any other painkiller I had consumed in the past. I hadn't been in contact with any in years, but imagined that not much had changed. The potency, maybe. I had never been careful about that before, either. I rolled the bottle back and forth across my palm so I could listen to the pills gently click against each other.

By the next afternoon, I was sure Pierre was developing a pill habit. It came on quickly. He would wake up periodically and nudge me for more. His legs seemed fine now, or at least he was using them with no hesitation. But I was worried about stringing him out for Daphne's friend. I told him we had to conserve them.

He did not like that. He looked forlorn, even when I petted him.

"We have to wait," I told him.

I went to my closet and found Daphne's hand towel and

tucked it under his chin on his bed. He sniffed it and whimpered. I petted him again.

"I know."

I watched him until he fell asleep, nose tucked into the hand towel.

When Daphne's friend came back in the evening, she didn't offer to pay the vet bill.

All she said was, "I told you he was a handful."

I wasn't sure I wanted to see him ever again, but I didn't think she deserved to keep him, either. I handed her the pill bottle and Pierre's food, and the bowls I knew I would never use again, in a bag, and watched her pack the car. I also gave her the hand towel. She looked at it and then back at me.

"Where did you get this?"

I shrugged, but I knew she knew exactly where I had gotten it from. She didn't place it in the back seat with Pierre. She took it for herself and thanked me in a way that seemed like she wouldn't call me again. I watched Pierre stare at me through the window as they drove away and I waved at him.

I crawled into bed and stared at the wall. I looked down at where Pierre's dog bed had been and noticed he had left a hairball behind.

24.

When I received his file from Bethanny, I saw that Lawrence was only at 50 percent on the PSAC. Bethanny had noted that Lawrence said he was always alone. And when I arrived at his apartment, I could tell that, besides her, I was probably the only person who had come to see him in weeks, if not months. He lived in one of those 1960s Los Angeles apartment buildings broken up into eight one-bedrooms. They had once been advertised as perfect for single people on the move, but Lawrence wasn't on the move anymore. He hadn't been for a long time.

I had googled him immediately after receiving his file and discovered that Lawrence was once a pornographer. One of those seventies San Fernando soft-core-movie directors—just loads of breasts soft-lit and bouncing across the screen and men with mustaches licking their lips in anticipation. Nothing crazy. I didn't even feel shy about going to see him after I found out. What was he going to say? *Evelyn, I was a pornographer*?

"You're Evelyn," he said when he opened the door.

"I am."

I found it a little exciting when I looked up his movie titles that there were a slew of women's names with *By Night* added after them. Terri, Toni, Wendi. Anything with an "i," basically. Stage names. I wondered if any of them were dead or dying, too. I wondered if his apartment was full of VHS tapes that he still watched regularly.

I also wondered what Lawrence's obituary would look like. Would it say B-movie director, or would it say King of double-D pleasure flicks? I thought about the story of the B-movie actress who was found mummified in her house. They said she could have been dead a year. Spiders had spun webs inside her mailbox for months before anyone bothered to look. She was somebody, until she wasn't.

Lawrence had been handsome at the height of his fame in the seventies. But now his entire apartment smelled like Vicks, and his white V-neck was soaked through with the ointment. As I walked in, I noticed empty jars of it in a Ralphs bag he had tossed beside the front door to be thrown out. There were some framed movie posters on the wall, but nothing too risqué. He needed a haircut and a shave.

"It's a mess in here," he said.

His trash was filled with used tissues and takeout soup containers—hot-and-sour was his favorite, he told me.

"I don't care that it feels like it's eating a hole through my stomach."

I noted the several bottles of Imodium A-D on his counter. And rows of empty orange pill-bottles lined up under the windowsill as if he was starting a collection.

Besides the posters, the few pictures he had on his walls all had the yellowish tinge of the 1980s. Nothing about his apartment felt current, inside or out. The tiles in his kitchen matched the tiles in his bathroom—a salmon-pink-and-black combo—and that was the only flourish to be found.

"I think I know where Bethanny left off," I said.

"She's great, isn't she?"

"I like her a lot."

"A beautiful woman," he said. "You are, too. It's almost unfair to think I'm leaving and all these beautiful women have just started streaming into my house again."

I laughed, because I didn't know what else to do. I wasn't going to be coaxing him to stay.

"I'm just old and invisible now."

He sat down on his sofa in a huff, and I took a seat in a recliner across from him. I noticed orange pill-bottles tossed underneath a side table near where he sat, collecting dust.

"How are you feeling?"

"Everything hurts. My joints, everything. I only got out of bed because I knew you were coming."

"Do you need me to get you anything?"

"Water," he said. "And applesauce."

I collected the mugs that littered the coffee table and went into the kitchen. The sink was piled with dishes; I thought about doing them for him. Everything was worn and chipped, and it was clear life had gotten away from him.

"I'll clean that up later," he called from the living room.

I opened his refrigerator and covered my mouth from the smell. A bluish mold had started its creep across most of the items in there. I took out a container of applesauce and closed the door. I turned on the faucet and returned to the living room.

"The place doesn't look big, but it's a lot to manage," he said, embarrassed.

"I understand."

I watched him drink and felt an urge to scrub away all the sickness and loneliness from this place so that at least he could feel a sense that things were a little under control before he passed on. He put the applesauce next to him for later.

"So I have to ask—have you explored all avenues?"

"She already asked me that," Lawrence said.

"I know, but I have to reiterate, in case there's been a change."

"I have explored them all."

"Do you understand this is completely voluntary?"

Lawrence nodded yes, but didn't say the word.

"Can you verbally affirm?"

"Yes, I understand this is my choice."

"Do you understand you can opt out anytime?"

"Yes. But I'm tired of the pain and I want to go, so don't worry about that."

I folded my hands in my lap.

"Did Bethanny finalize who would be coming by after you pass?"

"My ex-wife, Connie."

"Did you reach out to her yet?"

"We talk all the time."

"Really?"

"Better apart than together," he said, and smiled. "You married?"

"Not anymore."

"Doesn't suit me, either."

"Yeah."

"But then, when you're really in the shit alone, that's when you start thinking, *Maybe I made a mistake.*"

"There are nurses for that, I think."

"Not the same. What you want is someone who will lie down next to you, not afraid to catch what you have, and just be there with you. That's it right there."

"What you have isn't contagious," I said.

"No one wants to be around sick people. They don't want to catch the sadness."

He studied my face in a way that made me uncomfortable.

"But you do," he said.

"I just want to help you with your self-deliverance."

"I know. All you benevolent souls. *Selfless acts*."

"So we have to go through the tasks now," I said. "Seeking forgiveness, giving forgiveness, and saying goodbye."

"The letters. I started some of them already," he said.

He struggled to get up off the sofa, and I told him I'd get the letters if he told me where they were.

"Bedside table."

I went into his bedroom and found his coverlet on the floor. I made his bed quickly and noticed he had probably not washed his sheets in months. More orange pill-bottles crowded his bedside table. I picked some up and studied the labels, but none of the drug names sounded familiar to me, and the expiration dates were well past.

I brought his papers to him, and he tried to put them in order.

"Most everyone's gone anyway."

"It's still good to write them out. That way we can work our way to gratitude."

"Oh, is gratitude what we're working toward here?"

"So you can let go of these resentments before you go, yes."

"Sometimes I go back into the bargaining phase of dying," he said.

"I get it. It's a process."

"Is this how you're going to go?"

"Through self-deliverance?"

"Yes, with a hood and a gas tank from the party store."

"I think I prefer the Seconal route."

"Very feminine."

I sat with him while he wrote out his letters of forgiveness. He struggled with the one aimed at his father. He told me the top-line notes of his childhood and memories of America after the Depression. He told me about the first time he saw the Pacific Ocean. He walked into the water with all of his clothes on.

"Is that a memory you can't let go of?" I asked him, looking down at how the question was phrased on the questionnaire.

"It's one I come back to a lot. Everyone staring at me like I was crazy, but I was experiencing total freedom. I drank the ocean water. Can you believe it? I gulped it."

"That must have tasted awful."

"I felt such shame in that moment. Like I was some kind of dummy. I've done a lot in my life to be ashamed of, but that is something I can't shake. I had never been to the ocean before then. I didn't know."

"Shame is difficult to navigate," I said.

"These letters contain most of my shame."

"When it comes time to write the one to yourself, I want you to set yourself free from the rest of it."

I sat with him all afternoon, and when he dozed off I went and washed every dish and knife and spoon he had strewn across the kitchen. I cleaned the cups and wiped down the counters. I was overwhelmed with the desire to fill the apartment with loving-kindness.

I had to nudge him awake to tell him I was leaving, and he seemed disappointed.

"No night calls?" he asked.

"I don't think that's allowed."

"I wouldn't tell on you."

"You just want me to watch you sleep?"

"I don't sleep, really. Night is when I really know I'm dying."

"The panic sets in," I said.

"At a certain point the Xanax stops working and I have no choice but to ride it out."

"I know," I said.

"Will you come back?"

"Of course. We still have work to do."

He rubbed at his face and I saw dry skin flake off. His temples looked rough.

I called Bethanny on my drive home and she commended me on the progress we had made. She said she would schedule a follow-up meeting with him and let me know when to come back.

25.

During the Saturday session I'd gone to, Bethanny told the room that she was going to be on a panel at an afterlife convention in a suburb of Phoenix. It seemed strange for her to mix with the lineup of capped-toothed psychic mediums I found on the convention's website, but she said she wanted to clear up any misconceptions about what we were doing here and thought this would be as good a chance as any. Anyway, she had to make a living, and for five hundred dollars an attendee, I assumed there was more in it for her than just spreading our message of hope in dying. She said trainees could get a discount, so I used some of the money she'd given me for Daphne to pay for my ticket.

When I looked on the map, I saw that Phoenix was only five or six hours away on the 10 Freeway, with a vast desert in between. I don't know why I wanted to go so badly. Some days I thought Bethanny was a charlatan, but others I was sure she was the only person who held the truth about life. Maybe I wanted to see her out of her element. Or at least, out of our conference room with people always hanging on her every word. I assembled a case of wine, and clothes that could help me withstand the heat, and packed the car up.

The rooms at the Embassy Suites where the convention was being held had sold out, so I found a reasonably priced hotel nearby (with a pool).

It seemed like the right time to leave Los Angeles, which had started feeling small and dangerous to me. I was spending my nights looking up earthquake kits and go-bags. I was sure something catastrophic was coming. If I was in the desert, away from any faults, I could watch the catastrophe from afar.

On a Thursday afternoon, I got into my car and drove east. I waited to buy snacks until I was out of the city limits. I liked to see new things, so I saved my gas stops for towns I had never thought about, and now that amounted to towns in the Inland Empire that had been wrecked by meth epidemics. It didn't feel as unsafe to stop there alone when there was still daylight, but at night I always stuck to right-off-the-freeway truck stops for gas. The deeper I got into the desert, the more fanatical the billboards were.

Near Palm Springs, where the thicket of wind turbines crisscrossed the desert, black-and-white signs asked me to call God for redemption—888-THE-LORD—the white text so bright it nearly flashed. Call him and whoever was on the other end of the line would save you from yourself. Later, among signs for pawnshops and attorneys who supported the rights of divorced fathers, was a sign that promised a pill that reversed abortions for women who'd had second thoughts.

"What?" I said, astounded.

Outside a gas station near Indio, the light was fading to pink and purple against the mountains. Even though my windows were rolled up, I could tell the wind was a wild desert wind, the kind that made palm trees sway violently.

When I opened the car door, the wind did the rest, pulling it nearly into the car next to me. I watched the cars and trucks on the freeway glide back and forth trembling against the high winds. This was the kind of place where fast-food restaurants were lined up in a row next to gas stations that tried to edge each other out by the penny. Standing in the sun-bleached parking lot, where everything was covered in a thin layer of white dust, staring at the waning light of the sunset, I realized I had been here before. This gas station. Bobby and I had stopped here when we drove to Los Angeles, hopeful about our new life together. And, years before that, it had been where my mother and I had stopped when she helped me leave the city, drug-sick and depleted, to head east toward health and sanity. Now, years later, when I stood in the parking lot, I knew I was better off than when I fled the city for the first time, but I was still in a transient limbo. I tried to stave off these feelings of failure as I stared at this constant in my life, my crossroads a Gulf station covered in the sandy film customary in these struggling desert towns.

I sat with my car door open, watching the sun go down, the wind picking up, and forced myself not to put too much thought into how this place had seen me at my best and, more often, worst. But why was I looking to offer meaning to a meaningless place? I was passing through, yet my visit here felt like some kind of omen. It marked a passage of time at the very least.

Back when Bobby and I had crested the desert hills that would lead us into the Indio Valley on day five of our trek west, I was still feeling buoyed by the WELCOME TO CALIFORNIA sign that we had passed a couple hours before. I knew we were going to hit sunset in the valley, and I was not wrong. The God light breaking through the clouds crowding the immense sky felt like a cinematic homecoming. Dramatic in all the right ways, enough for me to lean over and say to Bobby, "It has to be a sign, no?"

Bobby just nodded, making me feel saccharine all of a sudden. When we pulled off for gas, parking where I stood now, I had stared up at the sky as the clouds turned gold first, then pink, and then purple and red. Here was the place where I felt I could finally see everything stretched out in front of me—sky no longer obscured by high-rises and cranes. I had been suffering back east and I knew I had to leave, with or without Bobby. I had gone to see a woman who had me lie down on a mat while she tried to catch vibrations coming off my body. She said, "You need sky."

"I know," I said.

All she saw radiating off of me was desert. White sand, yellow tufts of sagebrush, a bright endless sky of blue. I needed to be able to climb mountains and look down at wide expanses, city lights, and a hint of ocean in the distance. I knew I had to go back to L.A., but I was afraid to push for it. It was a city that had nearly done me in. A place my mother had had to scoop me up from, drag my belongings from my apartment into my waiting car, filling it until we could hardly see out the back window, and then demanded that I drive. We launched through the city streets and down the 101, both of us crying, as we left the city. I was sure I would never return; she was aware she was performing some kind of lifesaving mission. She was only partially successful, because I had found a way to come back that seemed safe. I was anchored by someone else who could make sure I would not go astray again.

ABOUT AN HOUR after I left Indio, back on the road to the convention, my mother called to say my father's drinking had gotten worse. This was not surprising, but it still gave me a jolt. I had hours of driving ahead of me in which to piece together how this could be happening again.

There had been an uneasy truce in our house after he was hospitalized a second time, only six months after his first, just a few months after our family trip to the desert. The first time he had been hospitalized had just seemed like bad luck, though years of hard drinking often have an inevitable end. No one would believe that he of all people could drink himself to death so quickly. It was an admirable attempt, but it did not stick. He had lost forty pounds in a matter of weeks. And that's when my mother and I learned the functions of organs we had never had to think of before. I could not recognize him. He was not just thinner but older. No longer the fierce antagonist in my life, he was just an old man, even if he wasn't quite yet. He was in the hospital long enough to detox, but it didn't last.

He said he was going to sip slowly, thinking it was the tenacity with which he drank that nearly did him in, not the quantity.

A few weeks after his first hospital discharge, we sat outside in the dark watching a soundless lightning storm together, the kind that rolls into Western towns quickly to cause a ruckus before blowing out just as quickly—flat land as far as you can see, and no mountains to stop it. My mother was scared of the storm and had gone inside, but my father and I prided ourselves for being brave against God's elements.

Every few beats the clouds above us lit up white and we could feel the electricity in the air. We loved watching the lightning skip horizontally from cloud to cloud. I tried not to look at his quiet sips, just like I tried not to hear the opening of each can. I concentrated on my own drink instead, the glass crowding with beaded sweat. I knew the bad thing—yet another hospitalization, or worse—was on the horizon, and it didn't need to be said. But I did.

"Why are you doing this?" I asked.

"What?" he said, though I was sure he knew what I was talking about.

"Drinking again."

He was quiet for a while, really thinking about it.

"I want to die first," he said.

I couldn't see his face and he couldn't see mine, but if he had he would have seen that he had knocked the wind out of me.

"What do you mean?" I asked, barely able to contain my rage.

He nodded toward the house—to the living room, where my mother sat watching TV—and said, "I want to die before her."

It was so simple, his announcement of his death plan, and carefully thought out, too. It was so obvious that it hadn't even occurred to me.

"I can't tell her, but I can tell you, because you can take it," he said.

"No, I can't."

"You can, you're strong. I'm not. I don't want to do it anymore."

"You have to do it. We all have to do this."

"I'm tired, Evelyn."

He choked up when he said it.

"I'm so tired of doing this," he repeated.

What was I supposed to say? I couldn't tell him he didn't feel this way or didn't have a right to.

"I want you to take care of her."

We sat in silence and watched the lightning bolt jump from cloud to cloud, erupting over us without a drop of rain, and then the thunder began and my mother called for us to come inside. I didn't want to be the only one to know how badly he wanted to die. But I was.

26.

As I crossed into Arizona, I thought about how, when he went into the hospital for the second time, it felt like a relief. I no longer needed to wait for the bad thing to happen. He was once again nearly successful in his plot.

When I found him in the hospital room, he was in a gown, covered in cuts and bruises, his index finger swollen. He had lost weight again, become grayer, no longer salt-and-pepper-haired. He smiled at me. He didn't look like he was dying at all, though his voice was weak and gravelly as he waved his finger around to show me the damage. He had slipped on rocks by their house and hadn't even tried to break his fall, because he had been too busy protecting his glass full of whatever he was drinking. We laughed at this fact, like it was obviously absurd. He was nothing if not consistent. The gashes on his legs were trying to scab over, and my mother told me they had happened days before his admittance into the emergency room. I stared at them both and he shook his head.

"I'm fine," he said.

"You're in the hospital," I said.

"Well, I don't want to be here. Ask them if I can go home."

"You're not even on solid foods yet," my mother screamed.

She told me it was time for me to take over. She did not want to be here anymore, to be his caretaker. That was his role to play for her, not the other way around.

"How about you drink some water," I said.

"He has an IV for that," my mother said.

Every few seconds, a moan would erupt from a room nearby. Hospitals were full of moaners, the aggrieved.

"Hello?" a woman in a room nearby said, over and over again. I wondered why the nurses didn't go to her, try to calm her down. But when I went out to the hallway to peer into the room, the room of unrelenting hellos, I saw her hanging off the side of the bed. At first she didn't notice me and kept on with her chants. And then, when she noticed me, she said, "Help me."

But I didn't. Instead, I just stared at her.

"Can you help me?" she asked.

I didn't move. I didn't say a word. I turned around and walked away.

"Hello?" she said.

From a nearby room I heard a man respond with "Yes?"

She had found a mate in her chant. I walked closer to the man, who kept responding yes on cue to her hellos. They were strange songbirds among the beeps and chatter from the nurses' station.

"Hello?"

"Yes?"

"Hello?"

"Yes?"

On and on it went, a spooky incantation.

I looked into the room and saw a man who looked as disheveled as the woman begging for help. An older man, he was uncovered, and looked insane, or at least like he had come from somewhere far worse than this hospital. They both looked like regulars.

I stared at him from the doorway, and he didn't acknowledge me. He just blinked and said, "Yes?" when the woman next door prompted him.

This hospital was full of weirdos, lost people, families huddled around someone lying as flat as a board, surrounded by beeping machines, or nervously watching their loved one drink and eat from the same pink plastic dinnerware that can be found in hospitals everywhere.

I walked back to my father, to his room, which he was sharing with someone I could only see parts of from behind a curtain. When I sat down, my father motioned for me to come closer to his bedside.

"Did you see this guy?" my father whispered to me, motioning to the other side of the curtain. I leaned over and looked at the man lying there. He was about my age, and also covered in cuts and bruises. He was blasting Maury Povich and smiling at the TV.

I looked at my father and he whispered, "He's a real loser."

He and my father looked like they had been in similar fights, perhaps with each other, and yet my father was still able to retain a superiority complex.

"He's detoxing," he said.

"So are you," I told him.

My mother huffed. We did not talk about the mechanics of his disease, not now, not ever. In fact, he had been so vague with the nurses and doctor that they looked at me blankly when I asked about his withdrawal symptoms. It shocked me to the point of anger.

"His pancreas is shutting down," I yelled at them. "That doesn't happen overnight."

In the background, the songbirds kept cooing to each other:

"Hello?"

"Yes?"

Their voices echoed and bounced through the hallways, no one answering their songbird calls.

The thing about my father is that he's always been charming. The nurses told me he was their favorite patient. They even said they wished he could stay. This was why my mother couldn't stand to be in the hospital with him. Drinking had turned him into a liar. When I came back to see him the next day, his finger was even more swollen.

"Have you asked anyone to X-ray you?" I asked.

"They would know if there was something wrong with it," he said. "They put ointment on my legs. Ask Lindsay. She's the nurse."

Of course he was already on a first-name basis with all the nurses.

His swollen finger looked like a snail without a shell. I couldn't find Lindsay, but an older woman came into our room and passed by wordlessly. She was going to see the loser, my father's roommate. She looked as distraught as I did. It was clearly not the first time she had visited her son in the hospital. I could see the shame radiating off of her, and I understood it.

"I'm bored here. And his TV's too loud."

"Do you want me to tell him to turn it down?"

"No, don't talk to him," my father said.

It seemed irrational for my father to be giving me commands at the moment; it was as if he was worried we might hit it off and he'd be stuck with the loser forever.

I listened to his mother ask him questions—Did he eat? Was he still hungry? Did anything hurt anymore?—while she tried to fold his blanket. His answers came in grunts, and a nurse, maybe Lindsay, whisked by us and onto the other side of their curtain partition. I thought about how torturous it would be to be my father's roommate here, about entire vacations ruined by his snoring. I was sure the man had unkind things to say about my father, too, especially when he was wheeled past us on his hospital bed and hardly looked in my father's direction. My father leaned up to see him go, as if jealous of his jailbreak.

"Where's he going?" my father asked.

The nurse looked at him and said, "Surgery," and winked.

What the hell was wrong with everyone here? I wanted to know. No one seemed to understand the severity of the situation but me.

"Do you like my socks?" my father asked me.

They were yellow, like chicks, soft and fuzzy, with traction on the bottom so he wouldn't fall.

"Are you going to steal them when you go?" I asked.

"I think they're free with the stay."

"You could have just bought them at the store and saved yourself the trouble."

"I had a nightmare about you last night and realized we're the same person," he said.

I looked at him for a moment, waiting for him to say more. He didn't.

"What was it about?" I finally pressed.

He shook his head and crossed his arms. I glared at him, angry he was withholding some key thing about me from myself.

"What was it about?"

"I don't want to say. But it scared me."

He looked at me and said, "I'm going to miss you so much."

"I'm here with you. I'm not leaving."

"That's not what I mean."

We sat quietly for a while, staring at the wall, into space. He was not dying yet. He would be fine, or as fine as he could be, and we would have to wait for the inevitable all over again once they let him out of the hospital.

When he was finally discharged, after what seemed like hours, my father brought me back into the stained-glass corridors of the Catholic hospital I had wandered through while my mother received chemo treatments years before. The sunlight shone through them as we rounded the corner on our walk to the parking lot. He trailed after me, as if in trouble. I remember spending my teenage years here, peering into the chapel to watch the shuddering backs of weeping people. I turned to him, though, because I wanted to hurt him, and said, "Look where you brought me back to."

I wanted him to remember, because he had spent the last two decades trying to forget.

As I drove through the Arizona desert, I thought about all of this, memories flooding back to me, memories that provided a template for my future. The kind of life tremors that had caused me to seek out Bethanny. The sun had gone down, and large bugs filled the desert air, quickly and quietly splattering my windshield as I headed east. I was getting tired, and I was still two and a half hours away from the convention. I had watched the sunset in my rearview mirror and wanted to see the last bits outside of my car, so I pulled onto an exit that led to nowhere—a sharp, straight asphalt line into the desert expanse—and turned off the car. The light formed a half-moon on the horizon; everything else was perfectly dark. There were no buildings out here, though I had parked next to an inexplicable construction site with a few empty cars and no one in sight. It would eventually be another gas station beckoning drivers. But now it was nothing, just a caged-off square with its windscreen already in tatters from the desert dust-ups. A thin line of red and white lights pulsated on the freeway in the distance, and I began to scream into the wind.

I screamed until I was hoarse. No one came to find me. No one came to stop me. Then I got back in my car and pulled back onto the freeway.

27.

I don't know what I was expecting the convention to be like, but all around me stood baby boomers in golf attire, or sensible wedges for seniors, looking starry-eyed, with lanyards that said SPIRITUAL ENDINGS WEEKEND 2019, their names in bold. Outside, the misters were on full-blast, as they often were in the summer months deep in the desert, but they couldn't do much against the heat inferno, and each time a new name-tagged attendee entered the lobby we were met with a furnace blast of hot air.

That they all would be comfortable enough to identify themselves so blatantly made me nervous—these were not casual seekers. Each person looked like someone's mother or father, or someone's grandmother or grandfather, and I could only assume they were all here because they were afraid to die. The parking lot was full of cars with license plates from different states, and it occurred to me that, just like me, these people had traveled to see "experts" who could tell them what the afterlife would look like. And, even more dire, they wanted help communicating with their dead loved ones.

Mediums lined up on panels to pick people out of the few hundred who had gathered in the carpeted ballroom of the fading Embassy Suites, which featured a pool and golf course within steps of the conference rooms. It was a one-stop shop for boomers. The crowd was mostly women, and something told me their husbands had stepped out onto the golf course, older white men in ball caps perfecting their swings while their wives tried to connect with people they loved who had passed on. There were pairs, too, husband-and-wife teams who had lost family members abruptly—daughters or sons—and desperately wanted to know if they were all right.

Books were set out on tables in the lobby adjacent to the ballrooms, so attendees could buy any number of self-published tomes about near-death experiences, pick up brochures for conservative talk-radio stations or AM radio shows that trafficked in conspiracy theories, or books about alien encounters. I had thumbed through some and noticed that the books mostly had the same kind of glossy covers featuring a waning sunset and Comic Sans font. Boomers crowded the tables and handed over crumpled cash before shoving their books into tote bags provided by the event organizers. A nearby room was filled with brightly colored silk ponchos, mystical print-adorned billowing lady-tops, and an array of overpriced Southwestern jewelry that had been manufactured in China. I made my way among anxious seniors looking through the daily agenda and complaining about panel overlap.

The morning event was a man who said he had a Ph.D. in something I didn't catch. Dr. Brauer wanted to hypnotize us—two hundred people, sitting in ballroom chairs close enough together that our arms were touching, hyped up on all the possibilities that lay before us. I didn't know if I should stay or flee when he said he was going to take us through the three worst moments of our lives, in order to turn them into teachable moments for new growth opportunities.

I scanned the group to see if anyone else felt my apprehension, but everyone seemed eager to participate. Even more, they looked like this was exactly what they were paying hundreds of dollars for. It was a kind of grief-immersion therapy. This all felt antithetical to the work Bethanny was doing. Yes, she wanted us to face our grief, our clients to look at death without fear, but not like this. So why was I here?

Daphne's death had dislodged something in me, and I was looking for new avenues for grief management.

I was sitting next to Philip, in his Hawaiian shirt, who told me he was there with his wife, Chelsea, newly retired and loving the Scottsdale lifestyle. A man in his sixties who had introduced himself as Walter when he sat down on my other side said he had never done anything like this before, though he admitted he did like going to Sedona, because it felt like a spiritual place where he could be himself. They didn't drive around the country in RVs, but they were wanderers nonetheless. It appeared retirement gave them nothing else to do but search.

Dr. Brauer told us to close our eyes and take deep breaths. "I want you to walk along a path. It's right there in front of you. Don't be scared, just start walking," he said. "Feel the mist on your skin."

I closed my eyes. I wanted to feel the mist.

"You're walking through the most beautiful garden you've ever seen. And you come upon an intricate door. Behind this door is the first of your trials. Behind this door is one of the worst things that have ever happened in your life. Now open the door."

I opened the door. Through my young eyes I could see

people idling around in my parents' bedroom. I didn't feel safe here, but I could tell no one noticed me. At that age, I was just hitting waist height on adults. Through hushed voices, I could tell there was something wrong, but I didn't know what. I just saw my father's feet first, the shoes he always wore. My mother was balanced over him, trying to wake him up. She called his name over and over again and he looked dead.

No one stopped me when I went to his bedside, but I watched as she shook him, while the other men in the room stood by, uncertain of what to do, but not wanting to intervene. Why were they standing there, then? Why not leave my family to their private shameful moment?

"Now close that door and leave the past in there. Walk down a pathway and don't look back," Dr. Brauer said.

I heard sniffles all around me, and it went on like this, nearly all of us crying, Dr. Brauer leading us down paths, through doors leading to our personal traumas—through sickness, death, and despair—our sniffles growing louder as we went on our collective journeys.

"Walk down the misty path until you find yourself at another door. Don't be afraid. Open it."

I hesitated, but I finally opened a new door. I saw myself driving through flat landscapes. I saw the horizon punctuated with natural-gas flares piped up from the ground where oil was being drilled for. The horizon was full of these tufts of fire shooting into the sky. I saw myself turning off on a ranch road and trying to get closer to the flares. I watched the oil-field workers watch me as I stared at the flares from the side of the road, careful not to cross beyond the NO TRESPASSING sign. From far away the flares looked ethereal, mixing with the stars, but close up they just looked industrial.

Moments later I watched myself driving into a snowstorm through the nothing town of Jal, New Mexico. My heater wasn't working too well even as I turned it all the way up. I pulled a blanket around my shoulders and saw signs for Loving and Whites City.

In Whites City I asked a stranger to take a picture of me in front of a giant green alien guarding the gift shop. It was snowing, and I had found my jacket in the trunk. I still looked at the picture sometimes, but I don't remember what I was thinking when it was taken.

Dr. Brauer told us to dig deeper, and a new memory flooded in. I felt cold, and I could hear water dripping. I was in a group of a dozen people, and we were walking single-file, holding lamps, until we reached an open cavern. I knew where we were. The woman leading told us to stop and face her. She told us we were in the darkest part of the cave.

"The only life down here is you and bats. And whatever organisms are in the water dripping down."

I had gone alone to see the deepest cave in America. We walked past light installations highlighting the most beautiful natural wonders I had ever seen—gypsum chandeliers and lemon-yellow sulfur cave pearls—but I was here to feel total darkness.

The guide warned us we might experience vertigo from what we were about to do next. She said, "If you're prone to dizziness you better sit down."

I wasn't, so I didn't.

"You might see light on the edges of your eyes, but it's just your brain playing tricks on you. There's no light down here. If you see hints of light, it's just that your brain can't accept what's happening. That's when people freak out."

There were murmurs around me, and I couldn't tell if they were happening in the ballroom or in my memory.

"Turn off your lanterns now."

We did what we were told and I stood in total darkness. "Don't freak out," the guide whispered again.

"Is this what death feels like?" I asked.

"Wouldn't that be nice," the guide answered back.

In total darkness, my eyes didn't reach for light, but my ears were filled with the sound of my heartbeat. I fought the urge to fall backward. I tried to keep breathing as my heartbeat became deafening. I thought about Daphne in her casket, plunged into total darkness. I thought about the weight of all that dirt on her. I realized that I didn't know where she was buried. I became worried she was having trouble breathing under all that dirt.

Thinking about all of this made it hard to breathe. I wanted to dig her out. I wanted to pull her out of total darkness, get the dirt out of her mouth. I reached for my own mouth, hoping to pry open my airway. I gulped at the air, trying to get it into my lungs. Instead, all I felt was dirt filling my throat and esophagus.

"Wake up. It's okay," Walter whispered, rubbing my hand. I opened my eyes, gulping the stale ballroom air, and blinked at him.

"I'm okay. I'm okay."

"Powerful," Walter said.

I clutched my throat and chest as Dr. Brauer coaxed us back. I saw everyone else wiping their eyes. They looked around, possibly embarrassed at the intimacy of the experience and their vulnerability in front of strangers. I was in such discomfort that I kept my eyes downcast: afraid someone might see how out of it I felt, my eyes full of tears. But the people around me seemed momentarily fixed—elated, even. Like they had been relieved of some burden. I did not feel relieved. I felt worse, like something had been unlocked and I couldn't push it back down. I searched my purse for tissues, knowing there weren't any in there. I wanted everyone around me to get up and leave so I could, too.

28.

There was to be a buffet dinner in the evening, with psychic mediums who could help us talk to people on the other side. This included Guy Roberts, the headliner of the convention, who had been greeted with cheers during introductions on the first morning. He was Botoxed and hair-plugged, and he made it clear to us that he didn't need to be here—he *wanted* to be here. When the woman leading the introductions asked him how long he had known he had *the gift*, he laughed as if the question was beneath him and said, "My whole life."

Though I had paid in advance and chosen the brisket dinner, I couldn't stay. Instead, I went back to my hotel, happy to be far away from the throng of retirees rushing upstairs to get ready for dinner. I stripped down and pulled on a bathing suit and went to the pool to float. I wanted to fill my lungs with as much air as possible. Misters blasted down on me as I stared up at the sky. I felt no closer to solace here. Instead, the hours of PowerPoint presentations about what happened on the other side and astral planes and higher levels of consciousness only allowed my despair to set in fully. The pool did nothing to cool down my body; I felt myself sweating through my suit.

I wasn't sure how I was going to bring myself to go back

tomorrow, but I felt guilty about the money I had spent to come here; besides, Saturday was Bethanny's day to speak.

I did not go to the hotel bar, because I was conserving money and I didn't want to talk to anyone. Instead, when I got back to my room I pulled out a bottle of wine that I had shoved into the mini-fridge. I had left all the contents of the fridge lined up on the desk—cans of cranberry juice, mini-bottles of liquor. Things I had no use for. I would put them back in the fridge to cool before I checked out. I only made it through one bottle before crawling into bed and falling asleep.

In the morning, I made myself a one-cup serving of hotel coffee, after inspecting the machine for use. There was a film of greenish tint in the water container, which led me to believe that the flimsy hotel coffee maker had been used only minimally. I was slightly ashamed that one of those users was me. But I didn't want to be late, so I surrendered to the Coffee-mate creamer and drank it down.

The smokers were already lining the stone benches outside, the heat already peaking at 9:00 a.m., the misters on full-blast. I nodded and tapped my name tag, noting that I was one of them. It appeared that they had all become fast friends at the banquet, pairing off and whispering about odd occurrences in their lives—the unexplained. I felt like an outsider already and worried that I had blown it by not staying for the dinner to meet Guy Roberts.

Because he was the main attraction, the large ballroom was a rush of people trying to find seats near the front. I imagined what other events that took place in these rooms were like: medium-budget weddings, sales conferences for lower-tier companies, and perhaps occasional motivational speakers who had photos with Tony Robbins on their website. This was not the kind of place where big dreams were hatched.

After I found a seat, I listened to the whispers of two women who said that Guy had sat at their table—their biggest chance to know the truth about the afterlife—and not only had he been unkind to them—"stuck up," one of the women said—but he spent half the time looking for someone better to talk to. Mid-conversation, he had stood up and announced, "There's someone over there I'd rather speak to at the moment." They were paying for this. They had bought his books. They were keeping him afloat, they said.

During his presentation in the morning, he smiled casually, as if he hadn't slighted anyone, and tapped on his controller to move his PowerPoint forward. He was the leader in near-death experiences, he told us. He was here to debunk death. There was an afterlife, and it was like America, but better. Better parks, better golf courses, rivers, streams, all the pets you loved and lost, and racial harmony. He laughed slightly when he said it, like he knew something incredible that we could not comprehend.

"I have evidence," he yelled at us. "It's science."

He paced the stage, and people clapped.

"What I want to do for all of you is provide a safe space where you can come out of the spiritual closet."

Everyone around me clapped harder.

"We are living in a time of fear. Fear of your own bodily death. Fear of the *process* of dying. Fear of living the greatest life you have ever envisioned. Fear of what's going on on the other side. All that fear hurts me. I can feel it. I'm consumed by all the fear in this room. And so are you."

He stopped in the middle of the stage and adjusted his microphone.

"Do you know that you can find out exactly what's happening on the other side if you really want to? Do you want to?"

People around me screamed yes.

"I've studied this stuff for years, people. And inside of us we each have something called a spirit phone. But most of us don't know how to use it. The people out there?"

He pointed past us, toward the door leading out to the rest of the world.

"The people out there don't even know spirit phones exist."

He shook his head like he felt really sorry for everyone out there, as people around me took notes.

"The problem with our spirit phones is that the signal isn't switched on. Our loved ones are trying to reach us and we're missing their calls. They want to tell us what it's like, so we can stop being afraid. *But we're not answering.*"

It felt good to believe that someone knew more than we did. That these experts were just withholding because it was obvious the masses couldn't take it. That made more sense than believing no one was controlling the boat. And so the boomers, women in bedazzled jeans and wedge sandals, nodded along. They wanted Guy to give them the truth. I watched everyone being taken in by his assurances, but I just couldn't buy it. I don't know what I was searching for exactly, but it wasn't this. This just made me feel sick and desperate.

He said that in order to get our spirit phones working we would have to do the work of getting to a higher astral plane.

"It's called being tapped in."

He was getting worked up again.

"When we get to the other side and see all the beauty there is to behold, we're going to be so overwhelmed we'll need to take a nap."

He got those kinds of transmissions from people on the other side all the time, he said. They took a long nap right after they died, because the journey was arduous. While they relaxed on the other side, we were left here alone to manage our grief.

"It's unfair, isn't it?" Guy intoned.

"Yeah!" people called back.

"But that will be us soon, and you don't have to be afraid!"

"Yeah!" people called out again, though less enthusiastically than before.

Someone's hand shot up in the crowd.

"Yes!" Guy said, pointing at a man in a Tommy Bahama shirt with a faded palm print.

"I died once. My heart went out for four minutes on the operating table. But I didn't see green pastures. So where am I going?" he asked.

Guy stared at him and shook his head.

"Four minutes. Wow."

"Where am I going if I didn't see pastures?"

To hell, I said under my breath. If you didn't see the green pastures of heaven you were obviously going to hell. A murmur started in the crowd. Guy knew he had to quiet it.

"You know, I want to tell you a little secret," he said, pacing back and forth.

People around me leaned in, waiting for it.

"There are endless opportunities for soul growth. Did you know that? And you're just not there yet, sir."

No one said anything. They were too busy taking notes. The man sat down, somewhat shamed.

"First, you have to find God."

He nodded like he had just told us something important.

"Did you know that?" he asked.

The crowd murmured yes.

"Then you have to know your real self."

He nodded along, like it had taken him forty years to figure that out. He pointed at the slide, which was up on the screen. He flashed to the next, which was a stepladder to heaven; each step had a word listed next to it, a new level to achieve on our path to soul growth so our spirits could be set free, with suggestions like "show compassion," "love others," "continue to grow mentally," and "learn to know your real self." We were all trying to get to the celestial plane together, but it would be hard work.

"Do you know what it feels like to die and come back?"

He waved his arm toward the crowd and asked if anyone else had had a near-death experience—or an NDE, as he liked to call it. Some people raised their hands.

"And yet you're here. With me, and us, knowing you've seen something remarkable, and still searching for answers."

"What's your name?" he asked a man in a striped polo and cargo shorts.

"Duane."

"Duane, you saw the white light, didn't you?"

"Yes, sir."

"But that's been documented, hasn't it?"

"Yeah."

"I'm looking for the evidence. I'm looking for the new thing. What else did you see, Duane?"

"I saw people I loved waiting for me."

"They were beckoning you in, weren't they, Duane?"

"Yes."

"They were trying to tell you it was safe to come with them, that the water was just fine—weren't they?"

The crowd, riveted, murmured with soft laughter.

"I think so."

"So why didn't you go? Why didn't you go yet, Duane?"

"I was scared."

Guy touched his chin gently and wandered into an aisle, getting close to us.

"Of course you were. Who here wants to die?"

He waited for hands to raise, but they didn't.

"I'm here to tell you that you don't have to be afraid. It wasn't your time, Duane. But now that you know that everyone you love is over there, it doesn't seem so bad, does it?"

"No, I guess not."

"See? That's what we're here for. Evidence and science."

People clapped and nodded. That was what we were here for.

"You know what they say about Steve Jobs on his deathbed," he said. "When he was dying, he said, 'Oh wow. Oh wow. Oh wow.'"

He paused for effect.

"He saw it. He saw what I'm explaining to you. It's like the movie *Avatar.* It's like here, but better."

He walked slowly, talked deep into his microphone: "Oh wow, oh wow, oh wow. How about that?"

A hand shot up.

"I've written books about all of this. Best-sellers! They're all outside, on the table, for sale. Oh wow, oh wow, oh wow. How about that? Don't you want to know what that's like?"

"*Yes!*" people around me screamed.

"I'm ready for questions. Who has a question? You."

He pointed to the woman with the raised hand and smiled at her. She was wearing red glasses to match her red Keds; lines creased her face.

"I'm glad you brought up Steve Jobs. He visits me often, actually. He's on a panel with my husband, my *deceased* husband, and Nikola Tesla. They are doing very important work."

Though I was close to the front, I got up to go to the bathroom, hunching down so Guy didn't see me leave. He seemed like the type of guy who would take notice of such things. I was getting a headache and did not want to hear the testimonials of the other people with near-death experiences. It felt like I couldn't get enough air.

In the bathroom, a middle-aged woman was fixing her hair—frosted and short, well maintained. She seemed flustered.

"You left, too?" she asked.

"I had to go to the bathroom," I said. "But I felt bad doing it."

"I couldn't listen to that again. He gave the same talk in Denver last month."

"You follow him?" I asked.

"He's very inspirational. I just wish he'd change it up. Give us our money's worth. Say something new." She looked at me and smiled. "It's your first time, isn't it?"

I nodded and smiled. She clutched a notebook to her chest.

"Take notes," she said. "Everything is important."

29.

Bethanny was no match for these dog and pony shows, and she was cast aside in a lightly attended smaller ballroom. It felt strange to see her in a subprime location, vying for our attention, whereas she had commanded it so easily in Los Angeles. I was so embarrassed for her that I did not even try to come up to say hello. I hadn't seen anyone else from our training sessions, either.

I stared at the ceiling of the conference room and noticed water stains lining the ceiling tiles. The banquet chairs were zip-tied together into rows, and the air conditioning was droning on, keeping the room too cold for the women around me, who rushed to pull on cardigans in various jewel tones.

These convention people did not want to hear about our methods or about grief management. They wanted to know how to harness their own energy, their own power to speak to the dead. To cut out the middleman, so to speak. I left her room early, too. I was woozy or dizzy, perhaps still in the throes of some kind of hypnosis aftershock. I wandered into another room, where a couple was standing together, nodding along to a woman onstage who was talking through a smile.

"I used to be a corporate HR manager. Could you imagine?"

She laughed at the absurdity of it.

"I was scared of my gift, a gift my grandfather gave me. I remember once, when I was a kid, I said, 'Grandpa, do you hear dead people?' And he said, 'Yeah, do you?'"

She smiled warmly at everyone.

"And even though I spent nearly my whole adult life trying to keep my gift under wraps, I finally 'came out' of the spiritual closet a few years ago. I'm a medium, damn it!"

The crowd cheered. At least she wasn't telling us that we had to buy anything to receive her gifts. The couple standing up among the rest of us was waiting patiently for her to refocus on them. And when she did, they clutched each other as if in a storm.

"You lost a daughter," she said.

"Yes," the father said, so quietly we had to lean in to hear. I took a seat.

"She was young. It was abrupt."

"Yes, and yes," his wife said. They were a handsome couple, not yet retirement-age, but gray from grief.

"I see something with the head. Is it something with her head?"

They searched for some clue that would link them to her, to the correct answer.

"Cancer," the medium said.

"Yes," they said.

"You know, she barged right in through a dozen spirits waiting to talk to their loved ones. They're all hovering above us—attached at the hip, almost."

I looked at the ceiling. It was a pale shade of yellow. I felt strangely compressed in my seat. I didn't want the dead strangers floating above us to attach themselves to me. Others looked up and smiled knowingly. The medium kept asking leading questions, and the bereaved couple kept answering as best they could until they filled in all the blanks for her.

"She wants to tell you that she's happy. That she's okay. That she knows this is hard, but you will meet again and it will be glorious," the medium finally said.

The couple squeezed each other. This is what they were after. This is what they came all the way from Salt Lake City for. She was providing them with a service, and I understood her function completely.

When she was finished, I watched the line of people around the couple grow. They were patted on the back. They were hugged. The medium hugged them, too. They were all sharing the human experience together as I watched from afar.

I left and checked out of my hotel early, certain I could not stay a minute more.

As I headed out of town and back toward Los Angeles, I thought about how my trips to the desert had become more frequent in the last several years, partly because I was hoping to find some kind of peace in it, but also because it felt like the miraculous was possible in places where no one else was around. As the vast expanse of parched land whizzed by me, I kept wondering why I was so intent on trying to pre-grieve. Why I thought it would work.

Was I also trying to pre-grieve the inevitability of Bobby's pairing with someone he would eventually move on to in a more permanent way—building a life with a new person in ways we could not? This included having children, of course.

As I drove, I was drawn to signs for a mission on a reservation. On the dusty road, I paused beside a cemetery hemmed in by rusted wire fencing, its crosses facing the mission in the distance. The sun had bleached most of the silk flowers and frayed ribbons that lined the sand-pooled graves. I drove on, and the bright white of the Spanish mission came into view. It was ornate in a way that felt out of place among squat trailers and desert-rough trucks. The parking lot was lined with vendors selling Indian fry bread, and the smell of hot cooking oil settled over everything. The license plates showed people had come from all over the country to look at the aging frescoes, and touch the saint partially enclosed in glass. They wanted to light gift-shop candles and adorn the church with them, let them flicker among the dozens of people kneeling and asking for something, too. I lit one and asked for the same things I had always asked for: to no longer be afraid, to have my grandparents watch over us, especially my mother and father, who needed protection more than I did.

There was a hill beside the mission where a trickle of people meandered from the church grounds like ants before disappearing into the rocks. People were sweating as they crawled up the rocky surface toward a cross high in the sky. The brave wanted to touch it. The less brave stayed closer to the base, where a caged monument to the Virgin Mary stood. An altar had various plaster statues of Mary lined along it, and another one sat higher up in the rock face. On the ground in front of the altar lay hundreds of coins, and hanging on the rusted fencing that kept us from touching them were dozens of weathered necklaces with medallions featuring St. Jude.

Places like this felt holy to me in ways that churches didn't. They were evidence of the randomness of the miraculous, and that filled me with hope.

I left the mission and walked into the desert for a few yards. There were saguaro cacti crowding the landscape, and I came upon one decaying on its side. It was turning black and folding into itself in the sand. I couldn't help but think its vein work looked just like a human's, proof that everything was interconnected. I looked up, wanting to share this discovery with someone, but I was alone out here, watching the faraway people line up to be one with God inside the mission.

30.

The case of wine I liked to travel with alleviated any kind of stress over finding liquor stores wherever I happened to be going. It was a habit I'd picked up from my father, or, rather, family vacations I had spent a lifetime taking. On my drive toward home, in a town two hours outside of Los Angeles, I found a homesteader cabin to stay in for a couple of days. I felt better after leaving Arizona, but still not 100 percent, like I was suffering from a hangover that I could not shake. The sun burned at the part of my leg exposed by the driver-side window, and my dashboard said the temperature outside was 105. I assured myself I would be fine, because it was a dry heat. The cabin rentals were cheaper in the summer, and from what I could tell the ones around me mostly stood empty.

My cabin was revamped, with painted concrete walls and newly polished concrete floors. There were still—as with many desert homes I stayed in—dead scorpions in the corners. I had gotten groceries on the way, so I didn't have to leave, but I had picked out two restaurants on the main road, just in case I felt lonely and needed to speak to another human, even if it was just to order a coffee.

I had been to this cabin before. I liked to come here when

things at home got too difficult, or, conversely, too monotonous. The cabin was down a dirt road that looked like a sandy wash, unincorporated and largely forgotten, save for a few cinder-block houses and chain-link fencing keeping the sagebrush in. It was near a house with bunnies.

I had first seen it when Bobby and I had come here on a desert house search a few years before. We had passed from asphalt to dirt road and a final street sign—Wonderland, it said.

Well past that was a burned-out trailer, recently charred, and all I could think of was meth, but we pressed on anyway, until we came to the bunny house. The bunny house had a razor-wire fence around it and a sign assuring anyone lost on their journey that the inhabitants had guns and would use them. What they were protecting was not their desert-bleached double-wide but the hundreds of rabbits in their yard. I slowed the car and watched them in awe as they hopped around in the sand, or sat in unmoving clumps of brown-and-white fur. These weren't jackrabbits, which I was accustomed to seeing bobbing around the desert. These were rabbits being prepped for sale. When I first came out here with Bobby, he had suggested we turn around when we saw the bunny house, but I said no. I liked it out here. Rain clouds formed in the distance dramatically, and you could see lightning storms dozens of miles away. There was nothing to stop the wind or water out here.

Now I found myself here again, but this time I was alone. I couldn't deny that it was eerie to be here by myself. I remembered a Realtor had told us about the hillbillies in the desert. How you needed at least two guns, because the police wouldn't arrive for at least an hour after you called. Bobby had said he didn't want to live someplace where he'd be forced to shoot someone.

I let myself into the cabin and arranged my things. The owner had left me a binder full of "Fun Things to Do in the Desert," and it included some places to take a walk. When I looked out the back window, I saw ATV trails lining the sand and decided to explore. There was a break in the razor fence that surrounded the property, as if the wire could really stop anyone or anything wandering the hundreds of acres of desert. A line of tumbleweeds had tangled themselves along one side, and, past them, sagebrush and scurrying lizards scattered across the land.

The first few lizards surprised me, but then I came to want them around. I liked watching them doing their funny push-ups. The desert was full of partridges with their little feather hats, jackrabbits, the shivering sound of a rattle (I didn't like that at all), and more lizards scattering among the pieces of quartz lodged in the sand.

There were other things, too. Unnatural things half covered by the sand, like pieces of sun-bleached carpet and scattered tires. The muted shine of broken bottles and rusting propane tanks shot through with bullet holes.

I pressed on, turning around periodically, feeling as though someone was following me, the dull anxiety of being watched. But no one was there. It was just me, alone, with the sun beating down and the lonesome cooing of doves. Here I thought of all the people looking for answers—those of us who could not piece together a sense of order in any other way.

The people at the afterlife convention wanted to hear that they were good, that they were okay, that they would be reunited with the people they loved who had passed on. And the psychics who had congregated there handed out assurances so casually: *Of course you're going to see your mother again.* And *Of course your son knows you always loved him. He's watching you right now.* The more I thought about it, the angrier I got. What shit, I thought as I walked past nubby shingles peeking out from the sand, pieces of porcelain toilets broken in shards by some rocks. I wanted to know who was leaving pieces of their homes all over the desert. How could it be that so many pieces so foreign to the terrain could have just ended up here? Was this wasteland once a subdivision of homes that the desert pressed over year after year? Where was all the life connected to it?

I finally came upon a single white, weather-beaten sofa sitting in the middle of a wide expanse of ATV tracks. There was nothing else around, but it was full of bullet holes, and some springs had begun to show. Though it seemed impossible that this had made its way out here, nearly a mile from any kind of visible road, the sofa looked like it had been put to use.

"A sex couch," I said, under my breath. Or worse.

I looked over my shoulder and walked toward the sofa and kicked around spent shell casings.

There were probably snakes burrowed in the coils by now, but I sat down on it anyway. It felt rather new, as in left in the last few years for sure, maybe even within the year—the desert aged everything prematurely. I leaned back and stared up at the sky. Sweat beaded down my back, and I had started to feel dizzy from the sun. When I heard the distant buzz of an ATV, I knew it was time to get back to the house. I didn't want to interrupt anyone's trip to the sex couch, but its presence reinforced my belief that anything could happen out here.

WHEN I GOT BACK to the cabin, I went about doing what I always did: looking through the items left behind by both the owner and previous guests. Usually, it was boring stuff, like half-used soy sauce, hot cocoa mix, and hotel-sized bath items. I went through my own things and found my weed pen, but when I attempted to take a hit I found that it had finally gone empty. A panic set in, and I started playing with my wedding ring.

I hadn't taken it off yet, but at least it was no longer on my ring finger. I wasn't trying to hold on to Bobby or anything; it just didn't feel right to take off the nicest thing I owned. After I went to Bobby's apartment, since I didn't want people to think I was still married, I'd moved it to the opposite ring finger. In the cabin, while I thought about how I was going to get a new weed pen, I moved the ring to my middle finger. A finger it did not fit.

I was also just about finished with a bottle of wine, so jamming the ring past my knuckle felt like no big deal.

I watched headlights pass over my cabin's front windows. I watched them train their light on the house for a while. I looked through my purse for pepper spray in case someone was going to try to get inside. The car finally drove away, leaving the cabin once again ensconced in darkness. I went to bed after checking every window and door twice. I waited to hear desert night sounds, but all I heard was the wind. This was the desert for me—vast and free in the light, terrifying and claustrophobic in the dark.

In the morning, I woke up to find my finger had become swollen, trapping the ring where it was. I knew I had to get it off, but after several tugs it became clear that it wasn't going anywhere. I was both hung over and in a state of panic, watching my finger swell and go pink. I judged my middle fingers side by side, to see if I was overreacting, but I wasn't. The one with the ring had grown wide and red. I rubbed butter from the fridge onto my finger, but the ring would not budge. My panic swelled; suddenly there was nothing more important than getting this ring off. I didn't even know how. YouTube videos on my phone told me there were several methods for getting a ring off. First I found Windex and sprayed my finger and tugged at it, but that did not work. Other videos I watched suggested icing your finger and keeping it raised, which I did for ten minutes while searching for the nearest fire department or jewelry store on my phone, both of which were listed as places to go to get rings cut through. But I didn't want to cut off the ring. That felt sacrilegious—the clearest indicator that I had not properly respected my marriage at all.

I was in no place to handle larger lessons here. I was just trying not to cry. Ice did nothing to get the ring off; in fact, it just exacerbated the pulsing of my heartbeat in my finger, and made me believe that the swelling was only getting worse.

I found a man on YouTube who assured me that he would be able to help me get the ring off. He had 650,452 views, and so I believed he had some kind of answer that had proved helpful to others. His method matched up to the directions that the American Surgical Association had posted on their own page. It involved dental floss. Their instructions felt opaque to me in the height of my distress, and so I searched out someone who could show me what to do. The man on the video spoke in soothing tones, neither downplaying my trauma nor making me feel stupid for making such a mistake. He said, "This may sound silly, but if you don't want to have your ring cut off you can use an item that is found in most bathrooms."

I ran to the bathroom and found dental floss that had been collecting dust. The man had made a show of sliding the dental floss under the ring and wrapping it all along his finger until he reached his knuckle, which he took great care in circling with floss until his skin wasn't visible anymore. He said the person in trouble was supposed to tamp down the swelling with the floss and use the end of it to pull the ring down the finger and over the secured knuckle.

I was distraught while tugging, not caring that I was ripping at my skin as I did so. I could not bear the thought of losing the ring any more than I could bear the loss of my finger. And though it felt dramatic, standing in a stranger's kitchen in my underwear and crying, finger haphazardly wrapped in someone's forgotten dental floss, it felt somehow appropriate in that moment. I could not handle any kind of loss, no matter how small or necessary, and so I tugged at that ring on my finger until it ripped through the dental floss, and my skin, and the swollen crevices of my knuckle, finally sliding off. I had become covered in sweat in the process. I sat down on the kitchen floor and put my head in my hands.

I knew what I was avoiding at home. Our divorce papers. The official end of our marriage. Bobby had found the lawyer and made the appointment after I left him. When I asked when and where I needed to show up, he told me that all I had to do was send him half of the lawyer fee over Venmo. It cost less for us to get divorced than it had to get married. Bobby and I discussed it all over texts. Six months after filing, we would officially be divorced. I didn't know what I was expecting, but this all seemed to be happening with little effort. I guess it was supposed to be a signal that we were allowed to move on. But I didn't want to yet. I imagined an envelope of court documents sitting on my doorstep, thick and heavy with reams of paper explaining what it was we were supposed to do now.

I DECIDED TO LEAVE the desert the next afternoon. When I finally arrived home, there was no catalogue of our shared life sitting there. Just a thin manila envelope with a double-sided sheet of paper inside, stamped by a clerk who made the dissolution of our marriage official. It was crinkled and puckered, as if a legal assistant had accidentally spilled water on it during her lunch break. A smear of yellow rimmed the top corner. I examined it, wondered if it was mustard, and realized that, for whoever it was who shoved this piece of paper in an envelope, my divorce paperwork was just another task, an obstacle keeping them from ending their day.

31.

I had turned my phone off while in the cabin and felt oddly dislocated when I got home. I only had one voice mail, from my mother. She wanted to talk about what we were going to do with my father's accelerated drinking. I didn't call her back. Coming back to my apartment was like moving in all over again, trying to find my place within this space. It even seemed like the fresh-paint smell had returned in my absence. Sounds I had gotten used to suddenly became frightening again: scratching on the roof, dozens of coyote yips activated by each ambulance that passed.

The morning after I got back, my back seized up in pain. First, my lower back was stiff and burning. To move at all was to induce throbbing pain. On the second day, my upper right shoulder seized up and I could not move my neck. When you're alone, there is no one to bring you food or pain relief while you are seized up in bed, immobile. There is no one to stroke your forehead and tell you that you will be okay. There is no one to provide comfort. In these moments of pain that felt both endless and debilitating, fleeting thoughts become dark. What didn't make sense to me was how emotional pain could become physical: how it could infect muscles and joints, inflaming them.

The space around my bed was becoming a place where things had been dropped and forgotten as I tried to lie very, very still for days. I only got up to go to the bathroom. I quickly turned away from my reflection—matted hair, greasy skin. Washing my hair was out of the question: I couldn't lift my arms over my head without screaming. I would groan while picking up my Brita, just half full of water. I could only move from one flat-cushioned surface to another, holding my arm out as I tried to sit down again. I felt my age acutely. I was going to stay alone forever at this rate, I thought. I would never be able to recover from anything. When I called Dr. Kassell to ask what to do, she suggested coming in to get muscle relaxers. I could not explain that I could not drive. I could not do anything at all.

In order to avoid any kind of self-reflection over the course of my deteriorating state, I retreated to fantasy. Mostly about what would have happened if I hadn't left Bobby. For one thing, someone would be bringing me Aleve rather than my having to hobble to the bathroom for it. He would order takeout, too. It was pointless to think about these things. If I called him he would come here and help me, but I had made it a point never to let him into my house. I needed a boundary. Somewhere, anywhere.

So far, we had been good at not having sex with each other whenever we were alone together post-separation. I wasn't sure if that was a good or a bad thing. We were stiff around each other, and he was careful not to touch me. I wanted him to touch me, just to see what would happen, if I would feel anything at all. But he never tried it. Instead, we liked to share memories and things we saw that reminded us of each other.

I saw Stephanie had a baby, I'd text him at a time of day that didn't feel too desperate—mid-afternoon.

Yeah, she's doing well, he'd say.

Stuff like that: life events.

My throbbing began to dull around the fifth day of being mostly bedridden. My lower back and shoulder had worked in shifts to level me, and now, as mysteriously as my pain had arrived, it disappeared again.

When I felt better, I offered to take him to lunch for his birthday. We hadn't seen each other in a while, and it turned into an opportunity for him to tell me about his new girlfriend. She was more aligned with the things he liked. They were "California woo-woo" things, as I liked to call them: being healthy, meditating, and embarking on a raw-food diet. I did not want to become sanctimonious about healthy living, but I had lived in California for too long to succumb to it. We were no longer the couple sitting at dinner looking away from each other. Now we sat across from each other engaged, laughing. Why couldn't we have been like this when we were still married? Maybe we were just better apart than together.

The stakes were lower, I guess, because I could go home by myself and not play out the same rote, fucked-up dynamic with him day in and day out. The kind of dynamic that accumulates resentments so deep that you have to leave. Resentments that seemed both petty and arbitrary after the fact. But they still existed, and their existence made the silence at dinner okay. Worthwhile, even.

But now we leaned in to talk to each other, gently mocked each other with the kind of familiarity that still hurt. I wanted to have someone to counter with, but all I had was Nathan. And he was a distant memory. I considered turning him into someone to be jealous of, but kept my mouth shut, afraid of being pressed for details that I would have trouble making up. I had come up with scenarios about him to masturbate to, but if Bobby asked me where he had gone to school or anything about his actual life I would undoubtedly stutter out the kind of lie that Bobby would notice. His scrutiny felt too embarrassing to risk. Except I had moved on from fantasizing about any kind of sexual encounter with Nathan. I had inserted other random men into bland fantasies of taking walks together, petting dogs together, quietly fucking each other in the middle of the night. It was as if something had muted in me during my marriage, during the peak of my unhappiness, and I could only conjure mundane devotional acts. I was struggling to find a feeling, any feeling, or access anything above lukewarm.

Bobby's new girlfriend was the kind of woman whom men used the words "easy" and "comfortable" about. Not as a negative, but as something to strive for. I was neither; I was complicated. I knew complicated meant too difficult to be worth it.

I didn't know what else to be.

As I drove home, my phone rang, and I recognized Bethanny's number. She told me she had the date for Lawrence's follow-up and was preparing his final exit, too.

"Can you help me finish the preparations?"

"Sure," I said.

"He said he enjoyed meeting and working with you."

I appreciated this type of feedback and said thank you. It didn't seem like she had seen me at the afterlife convention and I didn't bring it up. I didn't want to risk embarrassing her.

"By the way, we're having a potluck next Sunday, and I'd like you to come."

"Where we have our sessions?"

"No, Nathan's hosting," she said.

This was an opportunity to go into Nathan's house, rifle through his things. Maybe meet his daughter.

"Does he know you're asking me?"

"He said anyone from the training was welcome."

I had spent all this time avoiding him, and here was Bethanny bringing us back together.

"You sound like you're in a funk," Bethanny said. Her directness felt too personal, as if it was obvious that I was feeling vulnerable and it was radiating off of me, even through the phone.

"I'll go," I said. "I can make fruit salad."

32.

I got to Lawrence's apartment before Bethanny did. He called me punctual as he opened the door.

"How's the shame today?" he asked me.

"Mine?"

"Yours. Mine. All of ours."

He walked away and emitted a kind of thick giggle.

"I wanted to thank you for cleaning up. I always kept things together before—"

"I don't mind."

"I used to, but then I got over it."

He stared at me and mouthed the word "shame."

"Since you like cleaning up so much, I wondered if you could do me a favor," he said.

I told him sure.

"Would you cut my hair? I don't want to die looking like I spent the night on the street."

"I don't know how to cut hair."

"I can guide you through it. I have an electric razor to clean up my neck. We can use a mirror."

I followed him into the bathroom and could tell he had prepped everything for me. He knew I wouldn't say no.

"Will you bring a chair in here for me?"

I did as I was asked and he sat down on it. I looked at the electric razor and a pair of scissors he had laid out. He also had face scrub that looked like he had purchased it five years ago and never used it. I picked it up and stared at it.

"Connie used to cut my hair for me. She was a hairdresser, so she knew what she was doing."

"That's a lot to live up to."

"I'm not going anywhere fancy."

He pulled at the hair that had grown over his ears.

"Just don't break the skin."

As I stood over him, he held up a mirror and pointed out where he wanted me to cut. He dropped his head toward his lap so I could shave his neck.

"No one has touched me in years."

"What about Bethanny?"

"She holds my hand, but that's it."

"That's something."

"You don't realize how much you miss it until you feel it again."

I was concentrating on razoring away the thicket of small hairs that punctuated the nape of Lawrence's neck as he talked. Moles of different shapes and sizes crawled up into his hairline and disappeared. I stared at his creased skin.

"Cutting your hair is weirdly intimate."

"I know," he said, and laughed. "I like it."

"I think I got it all."

"I wondered if you could scrub my face, too. My skin is starting to feel like sandpaper."

I noticed the skin on the side of his face looked like it was pilling, or something like it. He said he would get dry patches and just rub, but the dead skin stuck to him in layers rather than flaking off.

I found a washcloth and wet it, smearing the face scrub around on it, too. He raised his face toward me and I gently rubbed his skin in a circular motion, going across his forehead first, then his temples, before crossing his cheeks and wiping down around his chin. He kept his eyes closed the whole time. I rinsed the washcloth and went over his face again, making sure I wiped away all the dead skin and soap.

"Done," I said.

He opened his eyes and looked at his face, touched it, and smiled.

"Better than the mortuary."

He took my hand and put it on his shoulder.

"You're a good girl."

We looked at each other in the mirror, and I noticed his eyes were blue and watery. He got up and slid my hand toward his crotch. I didn't feel an erection, but I didn't move my hand, either.

"I'm sorry," he said. "I don't know why I did that."

"It's okay," I said, finally moving my hand away.

"I'm just scared."

"I am, too."

It always felt strange to touch someone new. Especially someone who was searching for my affection. I remember trying to clutch my mother's legs as a child, not wanting her to leave me, and her pushing my hands away. Trying to get away. So I learned to keep my hands to myself and not to miss lingering fingers on my back. It felt like I had too much catch-up to do to let myself feel any sense of physical yearning for a person that felt safe. But it was always exciting to be wanted, especially when I was caught off guard by it.

Lawrence moved away from me and pulled his shirt off to shake out the sharp fragments of his shorn hair. His shoulders were bony, and the skin on his chest hung down in flaps, his muscle nearly gone. He noticed me staring and turned around shyly. I could see the outline of every rib in his rib cage as he leaned over. The entirety of how his spine curved.

"The only people who've seen me without my shirt off lately are nurses," he said.

"I can leave."

"Girls used to call me a beefcake. I could show you pictures from my physique pictorials."

"I'd like to see them," I said, even though I had already seen them online.

"I want them around me when I self-deliver or whatever you call it."

I stared at Lawrence as he surveyed his own body.

"What a strange thing that happens to us," he said. "The deterioration."

I could hear Bethanny knocking on the apartment door.

Lawrence said, "We don't have to let her in."

"Have you changed your mind?" I asked.

33.

A week later, I was standing outside Nathan's house holding a fruit salad I had bought at Ralphs, hoping no one could hear the doorbell so I could go home.

His building was a beige stucco monstrosity built in the eighties with the curved balconies and wooden railings prevalent in the Valley, places that had names like Rancho Park or any number of words followed by the word "Villa." And even though the Valley was fifteen degrees hotter than the city, the courtyard pool was empty. All around Southern California, apartment courtyards resplendent with forever-empty pools. I rang the doorbell again, and Lorraine answered. She looked surprised to see me, like she didn't know I had been invited. Or maybe I was just being paranoid.

"I love mango!" she said, looking down at my plastic-wrapped fruit salad.

"Good!" I said.

"Everyone's back there."

I followed her in and saw all the shoes lined up next to the door.

"Nathan has a shoe-free home," she said. He also had a plastic liner on the entryway, signaling that he was some kind of germophobe. Why did he want to fuck a stranger in a hotel room, then?

There were also no signs of cohabitation.

After I took off my shoes, I walked through his apartment. It had accumulated the volume of knickknacks and furniture, and evidence of life, that led me to believe he had probably lived here for twenty years or more. Perhaps roommates and girlfriends had come and gone, but he could still not let this place go. I wanted to know where his daughter slept. He seemed to have scrubbed any sign of a wife away. Maybe they had never been married. He suddenly seemed interesting to me again.

The carpet looked old, the paint faded. He had money trees all over the place, and a small personal gong in the living room. People were reclining all over his black leather sofas, which appeared to be evidence of post-college holdover. Debbie stood massaging some man's shoulders. She had found someone for herself, a boyfriend and an emergency contact. Good for her!

Nathan seemed to be the kind of guy who dabbled in Eastern cultures with abandon. Buddhism books lined his shelves next to Deepak Chopra books and, of course, Eckhart Tolle's *The Power of Now*. Nathan hadn't struck me immediately as a seeker—he didn't wear mounds of wooden beads on his wrist or any kind of crystal amulet—and yet here on view in his modest apartment was abundant evidence of his deep spiritual quest, which felt more vulnerable than anything he had shared with our group. He was just an ordinary lost person like the rest of us.

I went to the kitchen to deposit my fruit salad among the other potluck items: seven-layer dip, pasta salad, vegan hot dogs, three types of tortilla chips, and chia pudding. No one was in the kitchen, so I inspected the refrigerator, with its photographs and newspaper clippings and corny magnets. In the center was a photo of Nathan and his daughter. She was a preteen blonde with braces and long legs. I wondered what her mother looked like. I wandered out when I heard Debbie saying she needed to top off her iced tea.

I inspected a poster of a glowing orb radiating from a shadowed body and beneath it read: *"Drop the idea of becoming someone because you already are a masterpiece. It cannot be improved. You have only to come to it, to know it, to realize it. —Osho."*

"Fuck off," I whispered. I could feel someone staring at me. I looked around and saw it was Nathan. Had he heard me? Maybe. I felt like an unwelcome guest. He glanced at me and then went back to talking, but before I could turn around and leave, Bethanny had me by the shoulder.

"Everyone. Everyone!" Bethanny said, smiling, still holding my shoulder.

Nathan clapped his hands twice, and the people in his living room, chatting and eating hummus, settled down.

"Thank you all for coming. And thank you, Nathan, for letting us gather in your beautiful home. I wanted to take a moment and praise us for the work we've been doing. The help we've given to so many people. It is not nothing. And the sense of community we've gained from each other. That matters, too."

She smiled at me, and I could feel everyone staring at me: singled out by Bethanny in a way they all wished they could be.

"The identity we all share is the loss of still being here when those we love leave us behind."

Everyone around me nodded yes. I felt like the only person who didn't understand what she was saying. Why did she have to say things like that at a party?

"Those aren't my words, though—that's from *Walking Through Grief*, by the brilliant Christian Meyerson. Our identity can't help but be interwoven with what we grieve."

She leaned in and whispered into my ear, "Have you read it yet?"

I could feel her hot breath on my neck, and I wanted to lie and tell her yes.

"You will. You will," she said, before I could answer. She pulled me into the kitchen so she could fix herself a plate of food.

"I'm so proud of the work you did with Lawrence. It feels like you had a breakthrough," she said. "He really appreciated you spending time with him before he left us."

"He's gone?"

"He is," she said. "I'll give you your check before you leave."

"Thanks."

I started doing my breathing exercises to steady myself.

"I have something wonderful to share with you," she said as she led me to Nathan's meditation room.

It wasn't the first time I felt like I was being indoctrinated into a cult. California was ripe with meet-ups, healers, and healthy-living gurus. She always made us feel like we had a bigger purpose here, though, and so we were set apart from those simply searching for higher vibrations.

"Can you start a new client?"

"Alone?"

"At first. Unless you want Nathan to help."

This was my graduation. I could feel it.

She told me his name was Daniel.

34.

When I knocked on Daniel's door I assumed he'd be glassy-eyed, jaundiced, and medicinal-smelling. But he wasn't any of those things, though his house did smell like it hadn't been aired out in weeks. He lived in an East Hollywood bungalow that sat behind another bungalow that was cut off from the street by chain-link fence. Heat radiated off his cracked concrete driveway when I walked up to his door; I noticed the blackout curtains as I knocked. Bethanny hadn't sent me all of his forms yet, which meant I didn't have a last name so I couldn't search for him online.

When he answered, he looked very much alive, though he had the kind of dark circles under his eyes that made me believe he stared at the ceiling most nights, too. He had filled out the paperwork, and his prognosis showed no hope. He told Bethanny he was pretty much homebound—agoraphobic—though he could still do most things without help. The first thing he told me as I was settling in was that he didn't want to get to the point where he was bedbound or needed someone to help him bathe or go to the bathroom. He did not want to become a shell of himself.

I realized Bethanny had made a mistake putting us together

as soon as he smiled and ushered me inside. He opened the curtains so we could have some light, and I watched dust flicker through the new sunlight all around us. I could get a better look at him now.

He was forty-two and had cirrhosis. He said his name was on a list somewhere for a new liver, but it had been five years, and he told me he didn't have the kind of insurance that would let him survive anyway. The bags under his eyes and the gently hollowed-out cheeks were the only sign that he was not well. It did not seem like he had started to get rid of his personal items yet. The giveaways would inevitably happen closer to his death date.

He had a strong chin and other markers of good looks: green eyes (though they were sad), straight teeth, and a somewhat crooked smile. He had that musty, sweaty smell of someone who pulled clothes off the floor and wore them a few too many times. His hair was greasy and he needed to shave.

His house was small and wood-floored. I couldn't tell how long he had been living there, because everything looked haphazardly put together—too-small side tables and a round coffee table that looked like he had painted it with house paint himself—and the living-room walls were bare. I wondered if he ever let anyone else inside. A row of small cacti in glass jars with grimy water lined the front windows, and he noticed me staring at them.

"People pay for those, but you can walk around outside at night with a pair of scissors and get whatever you want for free."

We were sitting across from each other on his couch, he in gray sweatpants and a loose shirt, me in jeans and a sweatshirt. Though he had a window A/C unit sputtering out coolish air, I could still feel sweat dribbling down my back. I had a tank top on underneath my sweatshirt, but I didn't want to seem unprofessional by stripping down to nearly nothing.

We went through the death-directive paperwork, and I noted that he was an organ donor.

"I am, too," I said, as if that meant something about what kind of people we were. I was surprised he had filled out a good amount of the paperwork Bethanny sent over himself. I suggested we move on to more personal questions, so we could warm up to each other, make this all feel less perfunctory.

"What personal trait have you managed to overcome?" I asked.

"Starting off with the easy questions."

It was hard to ask that of someone you knew, much less a stranger who wasn't sure he could trust you.

I laughed and told him to wait until I asked for all his computer passwords.

"Can I give you those last?" he asked.

"We have a long way to get there," I said, holding up the packet.

"Overcome recently, or a while back, or what?" he asked.

"However you think it applies."

"Let me think about it."

I stared at the floor while Daniel thought about it. Sticky liquid had spilled across the floor at some point and it was now dried splatter, collecting dust. He followed my eyes and saw it, too.

"What trait have *you* managed to overcome?" he asked me.

I wanted to say my being here was overcoming something, but I didn't say anything.

"See, it's not that easy to tell someone the truth."

"I had to answer these myself," I said. "I know it's not easy."

"So what did you say?"

"I don't remember."

That was a lie.

"I thought you'd just come here and give me the pills and kill me. Or bring me a plastic bag. Not all this soul-searching shit."

"I'm sure you can find a bag in your kitchen. And I don't kill people."

"Not physically, maybe." He looked at me and smiled.

A personal flaw I had not yet overcome: wanting to seem dangerous.

We weren't supposed to lead them to an answer. They were supposed to answer with the first thing that popped into their heads. I looked up at him while he squinted at the ceiling.

"What's a personal trait I've managed to overcome?"

"Yes."

He sighed. It appeared that he had settled on something.

"My inability to forgive."

"That's a good one. I wasn't expecting that."

We weren't supposed to cast value judgments on our clients or their answers, but I was stuck on wanting to make an impression.

"Do I look like someone who doesn't know how to forgive people?"

"Not at all," I said. "That's just really big. Congratulations."

"You look like you forgive people for a lot."

"No, I don't."

"It's something I wasn't willing to do for a long time—you fuck with me and you're dead to me. But that gets exhausting."

"I get it."

He looked at me like he wasn't searching for my affirmation and yet here I was pushing it on him. I nodded and looked away. He made me nervous in a way that Daphne and Lawrence had not. Maybe because we were close in age. Daniel felt like a stand-in for every man I had known, and I still didn't have the courage to ask why he'd hurt people or why he was hurt.

I didn't want to manipulate him, really. I just wanted something from him as much as he wanted me to provide him with an exit plan that felt less lonely.

"We're here to learn lessons for something else," he said, "some other plane of existence, I think."

"What do you mean?"

"I think we pass through here and learn a lesson we're supposed to learn and then move on."

"This is an unnatural place for us to be . . ." I trailed off.

"In our bodies, yes. Why do you think we're in so much pain?"

"You're talking about our souls," I said.

"Don't make me sound crazy. But, yeah, I've been thinking about this shit a lot."

"I don't think you're crazy at all."

"We're just here for a human experience. And maybe that human experience is just to learn one thing. For me, it's learning how to forgive. Like, someone has a life with terrible parents or something, and maybe all I was supposed to do was learn to forgive them and maybe a handful of people who came after them. And that's it. Then I can move on to whatever's next for me. That was what I came here for."

"To be able to move on."

"Don't you think so? If we're not here to learn something, what the fuck are we here for? Dealing with all this?"

I shrugged.

"Really?"

"I really don't know," I said.

"Aren't you supposed to be an expert in this shit?"

"I'm not an expert in anything."

"What's next, then? Give me the next question."

"What day of your life would you like to live over again and why?"

"I don't have an answer for that one."

He didn't say anything else, just shook his head. It was too soon to ask. I had skipped ahead in the questions, because I really wanted to know. It was strange to watch someone go deep into their memory to try and piece together the story of their lives. Watching them hunt around for some best answer, decide what was too painful to hide, and even more painful to allow to the surface.

"Do you want to take a break?"

"Yeah, maybe."

"That's fine."

"I'm not the type of person who wants to relive happy days. Only the days that cause me the most guilt."

"Who doesn't want a do-over?" I asked, hoping he'd say more.

"Let's take a break," he said.

Even though Daniel was dying he still had color in his face, a warmed tan that made clear he still left the house occasionally. He went to the bathroom, and I got up to look around. His kitchen was the only place that showed any kind of evidence of his sickness. Near the sink sat half a dozen orange prescription bottles neatly in a row, and a pile of tissues brimmed out of the trash that looked like they were speckled with blood. When I looked at the pill labels, I noticed they were painkillers I knew well.

I heard the sink in the bathroom running and turned back toward the sofa. On the hallway wall I noticed pictures of him with women, maybe friends, maybe not, in vacation locales like Angkor Wat and snowcapped mountains far away. What was he like then? Where were these women now? It seemed as though there should have been a steady stream of mourners waiting by the door, but there was just me. There were also photos of Daniel dressed in sand-colored fatigues in the desert.

"Where is this mountain?" I asked, as he came up behind me.

"The Andes. I used to snowboard," he said. "I did a lot."

"It looks like it."

"I'm not some sad sack who wishes he got to do more. I did enough."

"That's good," I said. "Most people never do much with their lives."

I liked being antagonized by him. He knew exactly what to do.

35.

Bobby texted me later that evening and said, *I have a box for you.*

His insistence that I needed to retrieve an oversized mug and some small objects that I had forgotten about told me that this wasn't about the objects at all. I had been watching from a distance as he sent out sale notices about our furniture, and even some items he had bought on his own after we split. He said he had to get rid of them right away. He was redecorating, he said. *It's her,* I thought. As I climbed out of my car, I sniffed the air, hoping for a whiff of the jasmine or orange-blossom blooms that I associated with coming here, coming home. But the air only smelled of eucalyptus leaves drying in the late-summer heat. It would not cool down again until November, when you'd start to feel the slight sweat of night humidity again.

I'd left some of the things I cared about with Bobby because I didn't want them to end up with strangers. I was also leaving the memories associated with those items. When I walked up to the door of our old apartment, I was happy I didn't have to see my old neighbors again: all their windows were dark. Bobby gave me a small, neat box before I even came into the apartment.

We had agreed to dinner. And as we drove there, being together once again felt so familiar that I was thrust back into the feelings of being in a couple. Not buoyancy, but comfort. We were driving to the same restaurant we always used to go to, and when we sat down to order, we ordered the same things we always ordered.

His girlfriend was moving in, he said. I knew this was part of the deal. Not just his moving on, but also the fact that if I were to come to the apartment, our former apartment, it would look different. It already did, but it was his familiar touches, not hers. He seemed anxious about this.

I said, "But this is what happens in relationships. Women know what isn't yours, and they slowly sift those things out of your life."

"I know."

"I don't want any of the things back, though."

"Are you sure?"

I was, but it still felt like a rejection of our previous life together.

Though we texted each other quite often, she did not enter into our conversations. Instead, they felt like a space where we could still share time together. I never asked questions about her; I did not want to know. At dinner, she became a topic of conversation—and I was giving him relationship advice.

"Maybe you should have given yourself more time to be alone," I said.

"I know."

"I couldn't imagine living with someone again."

"It's hard."

"She'll want to get married. Then what will you do?"

We were two people who had gone through the same

trauma—divorce. We could speak candidly with each other in ways that non-divorced people could not. I knew I didn't want to date because I was afraid that someone would want something from me that I was unable to give—commitment, love, trust, an idea of a future.

"I can't get married again," Bobby said.

"I know. I know."

We shared this pain together. We both felt it.

Unfair or not, I felt superior in that moment. I was avoiding this pain by not participating. He was opening himself to be hurt and to hurt someone. I, on the other hand, was working hard on not feeling this loss, because I did not want to feel something that I could not recover from.

"In all of this I have discovered that I don't know how to be a 'we,'" I said.

"What?"

"It sounds simple, but it's everything that's wrong with me. I don't know how to be part of a 'we.'"

He nodded, and though I was ashamed, my eyes started to fill with tears.

"I have always subscribed to 'I alone can fix this. I don't need anyone. I don't need you,'" I said. "Because I don't know how to be a 'we.'"

I waited for him to say something, but he just looked at me; it felt like my tears were spilling over, but I wasn't sure. I looked away, because I couldn't bear to see tears filling up his eyes, either. It felt cruel that we had to be apart to have this kind of growth.

"So—what are you going to do?"

"I don't know," I said. "It feels big enough to even know that. But I don't know how to fix it."

"I told you that through our whole marriage," he said. "I never felt so alone as when I was with you. You wouldn't let me in."

"I just don't know how," I said.

Self-preservation is a funny thing: in order to survive, you do things that ultimately hurt your chance of survival.

"Just be honest with her," I said. "That's all you can do."

I drove around with the box in my car for three days before I brought it inside. I opened it to find the oversized mug that I had purchased for no reason, or with the idea that we would drink hot chocolate together. I don't know why there was only one. And some things we had picked up in the desert. Rocks, small bones of animals that I could not identify. Why had I spent so much time collecting remnants of death?

I didn't want anything in the box, but instead of throwing it away I tucked it into the back of a cabinet, next to other boxes he had given me—boxes filled with birthday cards and anniversary cards that he had held on to because he was more sentimental than I was; our wedding vows—both mine and his; postcards we had found in consignment shops that were already filled out with cursive notes from people who missed each other and spoke to us in some way. I was not prepared to open any of these boxes.

My phone lit up with a message. I reached for it quickly.

Daniel had texted a simple sentence:

Was that weird?

I paused, trying to figure out how to answer. Should I play cool and aloof or needy? I knew the answer; I just didn't know how not to feel like the latter.

What?

I saw bubbles forming and cascading back and forth.

I feel like I wasn't answering the right way.

No no you were fine. There's no right answer!!!

Yah ok. See you soon.

I stared at the few words I had sent and knew they were all wrong. I was generally inept at drawing out conversation. I wanted to send paragraphs, but didn't want to seem effusive. I questioned how many exclamation points I had sent. When I looked at them now, three felt entirely unnecessary. I imagined him saying "yah ok" with a cool indifference. But it felt meaningful that he was worried he had done something wrong and came looking to me for guidance. He didn't seem like a person who looked to people for advice. Certainly not women. He seemed like a person who made decisions without second-guessing himself. I decided it had been vulnerable of him to text me. It showed he had been thinking about me even after I left. I wanted to text him back, ask him what he was doing. But I couldn't figure out a way to re-engage, so I just sat staring at our messages.

In the morning, when I woke up, bright morning light flooded through my windows as I walked from room to room. The remnants of my night were lined up along the sink: a low-ball glass with withered rinds of citrus, an empty wine bottle, a wineglass fogged with greasy fingerprints, one dirty dish. A headache was already flooding my forehead from temple to temple. I took the wine bottle to the grocery bag that held my recycling and stared at the empties in it—an empty gin bottle, empty wine bottles for each day of the week, and a scattering of empty food containers—and dropped the new empty in with a clink. I reminded myself that I needed to be more efficient about throwing away my recycling, so it didn't look so desperate in there. I could smell alcohol oozing out of my pores. I hadn't felt this bad in a while. My hangovers had always been manageable—I knew just how far to go—but it had just been one of those nights when I didn't have an off switch.

As I walked around, I saw that I had left my windows open and my front door unlocked. I hadn't blacked out, but I wasn't used to being so careless, and the fact that I hadn't closed the windows and locked the door before I fell asleep worried me.

I steadied myself at the sink and looked out the window. Through the cacti and lemon trees that lined the stairs next to my house I spotted a curled-up coyote in the dirt in the yard next door. It was sleeping, and I watched it breathing. It didn't see me when it woke up and started scratching and yawning. It blinked and licked its chops and stared out into the hills. I stood there watching it—quiet, so as not to disturb. Hidden here, the coyote felt safe enough to wake up slowly. It got up with a flick of its tail and walked down the hill and through a hole in the fence and disappeared. As I watched it slink away, I imagined what it would be like to feel that safe.

36.

I texted Daniel on the night before we were supposed to have another session. I'd been thinking about what to say for two days.

I settled on *Is tomorrow still good for you?*

He didn't write back for twenty-six minutes.

Oh right. I forgot it was tomorrow. What time?

5. But if that doesn't work we can change.

No, that's good.

Before I could think of anything better, I sent a thumbs-up emoji.

"Fuck."

I threw my phone across the room and walked away.

EVEN AFTER OUR text exchange, Daniel greeted me with the awkwardness of someone who was nervous that he had overshared. We were doing something deeply intimate here, but we were strangers. He told me that in some ways it made this easier: I had only his side of the story and no one else's, to see if they matched up. Or to question whether he was telling the truth or obscuring the facts. We both knew that much of this process was up to him—including how much he was willing to let go of before he died.

"How was your week?" he asked.

"Uneventful, really." It was true but he also didn't know anything about me. He didn't ask, either, though I wanted him to. Before our appointment I had spent great care in deciding what to wear. I had a glass of wine. I shaved my legs. I bought an at-home wax kit, my first. I waxed my bikini line and took an electric razor to the rest to trim. I moisturized every last inch of myself after scrubbing myself down with a loofah. I had not done this for Nathan, but it seemed like something Daniel would notice and appreciate if anything were to happen. I put on a skirt that I knew showed off the shapeliness of my legs. I wanted him to be surprised by them while I asked him my questions.

When I arrived, his curtains were already wide open and I could tell he had cleaned. The house smelled like cheap floor-cleaner, and when I sat down I noticed the splatter was gone. He had shaved and washed his hair. The effort felt meaningful.

I asked him how he was feeling, if he had new or worsening symptoms, but he said he was feeling stable this week—stronger, even. We joked that maybe he wasn't dying after all.

"I've been praying," he said. "Maybe that's helping."

"It does. It will."

"I don't only pray for the things I don't have," he said. "I pray for all of it. Even what's happening to me."

"Me, too."

He didn't ask me what I prayed for, but I was doing my job of affirming his feelings. It helped deepen clients' trust and helped them let go.

"Was that going to be your next question, 'Do you believe in God'?"

"That's question seventeen. We're not there yet."

"Do these go in order of understanding or something?"

"Yeah, I start with softball questions about forgiveness and move on from there."

He laughed and said, "So what's the last question?"

I put my bag down and opened my binder. I laughed when I saw the question, because I had forgotten what it was.

"What is it? Have I ever killed someone?"

"No, it's 'What brings you joy?'"

He didn't seem to be a depressive, so this couldn't be difficult for him to answer. He stared at the ceiling and thought about it.

"Leaving things on a hopeful note—that's nice."

"There's more to it after that question, though."

"I thought just sixty questions stood between me and joy," he said. "And then death."

"Well, there's only forty. But no. We have to go through this binder."

"I should just snowboard into an avalanche, it would be easier."

"That's true, but also you wouldn't have died a conscious death."

"Are you sure about that?" he asked me.

"You said you care about your soul."

"I don't really want to cut our time short, either."

He sat down on the sofa and surrounded himself with pillows.

"I was thinking about your personal-trait question some

more. And I think that maybe I'm finally able to develop emotional intimacy with someone without wanting to punish them for it. Or hurt them for being too close. That seems big."

"That's a lot to come to terms with in a week."

"Sorry to all the women in my life. Too little too late, though, I guess."

"When it comes time to write letters asking for forgiveness, you can keep that in mind."

"What if they don't want to hear from me?" he asked.

"Then I can just keep them."

Sitting across from Daniel made me feel like I had learned nothing at all. Because his answers mirrored my own, and mirrored the way I moved through the world, I wanted to be close to him. But I knew how both of us would react.

He walked over to the kitchen as I stared down at my binder of questions. I was standing between him and an end goal, and I could withhold it for however long I wanted.

He walked over with a glass of water and lingered to look at the questions I had open.

"When are you going to ask me that one?" He pointed down at "How do you avoid pain?"

"I'm supposed to build up to that one."

"I'm ready for it."

"I have to ask it over and over again for five minutes."

He nodded.

"Are you sure?"

"Is it any more difficult to ask than what day you'd want to live over again?"

"Is it?"

"No. Each one brings a flood of memories I don't want to deal with, so just fucking do it. We're in it already."

"Fine."

Daniel sat down again near me, and we looked at each other briefly. I looked back down at my binder and flipped pages.

"We have to face each other to do this."

"So face me," he said. My skin began tingling.

"How do you avoid pain, Daniel?"

"Physical or emotional?"

"I didn't specify."

He looked around the room and nodded.

"Ask me again."

"How do you avoid pain?"

"Alcohol."

"How do you avoid pain?"

"Adderall."

"How do you avoid pain?"

"Fucking."

"How do you avoid pain?"

"I inflict it on other people."

"How do you avoid pain?"

"I find ways to be alone so I don't have to be emotionally connected to anyone."

"How do you avoid pain?"

"I look for people who are better at living with their pain than I am and I have sex with them, so for a brief moment I don't have to think about my own. And I feel stronger than them when I leave."

I don't remember what he said after that.

I leaned over to kiss him and he pulled me on top of his lap. I pulled my skirt up as I crawled onto him.

"I'm not sure it'll work."

"What?"

"I'm on a lot of medication, and I haven't done this in a long time."

"It feels hard."

"It might not last."

I kissed him again and said, "I don't care."

He tapped my back with his fingers and hoisted me up so he could unzip his pants and pull out his cock so I could slide onto it. He gasped and tilted his head back as I rode him. My knees ground down into his couch cushions as we fucked. He held on to my hips and came quickly. I jumped off him, suddenly aware of what we had done. I pulled up my underwear and looked around for my things.

"You don't have to go," he said, and though I imagined he had uttered that phrase hundreds of times, he couldn't even sound like he meant it.

"I don't know what I'm doing."

I could feel his cum getting my underwear wet. I didn't want it to dribble down my leg in front of him.

"Don't say anything to Bethanny," I said.

"I won't."

I packed up my things and felt him watching me, but he didn't move to help me.

I drove home and I knew he wouldn't tell Bethanny. I could tell he was accustomed to keeping secrets. I wanted to leave with the upper hand, but I didn't really, because I wanted to fuck him again so badly.

On my way home, I thought about how strange it was to be with a new person after being with the same one for so long. His penis was a different size and shape. I had forgotten about variation. I compared him with Bobby even though I didn't want to.

It made me miss Bobby for a moment. Not that Daniel's penis was any better or worse, it was just different, and the difference reiterated that I would never see or feel Bobby's penis again. I felt ashamed that this was the point that made me miss Bobby. That this was the thing that drove home a sense of loss for me. It seemed reckless to want to look at these encounters through a lens of love.

My sense of loss contained the following things:

That Daniel would never know that I left and called pharmacies on my drive home to see if they had Plan B.

That I considered buying it in a different neighborhood after calculating the probability that Bobby would be in line behind me while I picked up the Plan B from our pharmacy.

That I had taken it before, years before I met Bobby, and though I was more than a decade older, I still felt ashamed to ask for it.

That I provided my club-card number but immediately regretted it in case Bobby would receive coupons for emergency contraception the next time he came to fill a prescription.

I waited for the pharmacist and was surprised when she was nice. She said, "I know it's a lot. It will be okay." I wondered if she could tell I felt ashamed, irresponsible, or if I just looked like someone's wife who had had an accident with her husband. A wife who didn't want a baby. I admired her eye shadow as she talked, which was as expertly applied in various shades of copper and gold as any online video makeup artist that I had watched late at night. She just told me if I threw up within three hours I would have to come back to try again. That my cycle would be fucked up, though she didn't use those words. She made it seem like it was no big deal that I, an adult woman, had acted carelessly. She didn't tell me the inside of my uterus would come out in dark sheets.

I wanted to tell Daniel he owed me $39.99 for the trouble. I let myself have a UTI for three days so I could still feel him inside of me.

37.

Perhaps my inability to forgive myself or others stemmed from a frequent lack of compassion for how other people handled weakness. Because I was so worried about being hurt by anyone, I had lost the ability to see that maybe people who caused the most pain were also those in the most pain themselves. That's not to say that I didn't seek out hurt people continually. Even now I was constantly looking for a proximity to pain. I learned early in life to believe that my capacity for pain was higher than other people's. But that didn't mean I didn't also have a good childhood.

Once, my father said, "I achieved so much in my life—I worked, I was your father, and all I wanted was for you to thrive—but you'll only remember me as an alcoholic."

It felt like the cruelest thing I could do to him. To myself.

I wanted to say, "I'm sorry. I don't want to. I know you're more than that." But all I said was, "I love you."

To come to terms with gray areas is to begin to understand what forgiveness really means. I had long been flattening my father into just an alcoholic, but he was an alcoholic *and* my father. He taught me how to stand up for myself *and* taught me to cower.

I could have loved Bobby *and* have left him. I could fear pain *and* still seek it out at every opportunity. I could be smart *and* incredibly reckless.

So here I was, forcing myself, through others, to give space to pain.

What I felt more comfortable with was physical pain, because it was manageable and often didn't linger. What I found interesting was that when we were in training with Bethanny, the men always asked if the pain we meant was physical or emotional, but the women always focused on emotional pain when answering.

What I was most uncomfortable with was gaining acceptance that my father was actively dying *and* I still wanted him to live.

And so I participated in the fantasy that he was okay. That the bourbon was to combat his cold. That the stomach pains he complained about were not a sign of impending doom, or at the very least signaled a future phone call that meant I would have to fly to a hospital bedside again, if I was lucky.

And when he talked about the future, I listened, and I believed, just as I had believed in the future talk of others who I knew would not be around for longer than a season. I believed because I wanted to believe.

I DID NOT WANT to see Daniel again, so I had to run away from him. I *did* want to have sex with him again. I just did not want to piss off Bethanny. I didn't even tell her about what Lawrence did. No one said outright that something like this could happen, and no one shared situations in which they even came close. But when you develop a closeness with someone, it feels inevitable. At least to me. Or maybe I was just fucked up and couldn't understand boundaries. But none of this mattered, because I hadn't heard from Daniel.

I had a few overnight bags strewn about in various parts of the apartment, waiting for me to fill them haphazardly. They were called weekenders, but couldn't fit the odds and ends of my itinerant travel. Instead of heading back to the desert, I was going to head north, up the 5, before switching over to the 14, toward Lancaster, past Daphne's house and the now yellowed and withered poppy fields.

I briefly thought about Nathan and our hotel room as I passed the exit on the freeway. The pillows. The pool full of children. I was never going to be the type of woman who went for men like Nathan. But I also didn't want to be the type of person who always picked men like Daniel.

The two hotels that I knew of in Death Valley were booked, so I found a house deep in the rocky valley at the base of the Eastern Sierras. I hadn't told anyone I was going, but I had sent an e-mail with a picture of a ranch I found on a real-estate website to my parents. It contained a main house and stalls for horses on five acres of land. My e-mail said: "House I Want."

I didn't have the money for a down payment, and I did not know how to tend horses or live on a ranch. What I wanted them to say was, "Do you need money?" What I wanted to write was, "Yes."

They wrote back saying: "What if Dad helped you buy it? He has money. Or take our house."

They were starting to give things away.

When you are dying, you are invested in making sure the people you love are set up properly. Suddenly mothers want to make sure their daughters have found the ones they love and are on the path to marriage and children, whether they know they will be there to act as grandmothers or not. Fathers want their daughters to be safe and secure. My father suddenly wanting to buy me a house felt in line with this concern. He wanted to make sure we had an understanding that he was not all right with my living alone in an apartment after my divorce, with no discernible focus on the future.

It was both selfish and not. If he hadn't been rushing to kill himself quickly, then he wouldn't have jumped at the first home I had shown him.

The ranch had been on the market for over a year, and I didn't know the first thing about buying a house, but with my father's affirmation and assurance of some money to help me with a down payment, I slid comfortably into the fantasy of knowing that I would not be unmoored forever.

When my father did not approve of a man I was with, which was often, he would wave his hand dismissively and say, "Leave him if you want, because I will always be there to take care of you."

He helped me become a leaver. Mostly because he made it clear early on that no one would ever be good enough for me.

"No one will love you as much as I do," he said once.

He was my father, my protector, and my biggest tormentor.

"I know," I said, and I meant it.

THE TOWN IN the Eastern Sierras I found was built by movie studios in the 1940s or '50s and still provided appropriate fantasy backdrops for the Western ideal today. The fantasy was still sellable here, unlike on the other side of the mountains, which featured a different kind of seeker of God. The town functioned as a stopover point for a trail that cut up and down through the entire West Coast. Backpackers frequently crossed the street, looking for showers and one-night stays in the twin-bed rooms of motels that lined the road, which traversed the town on its way up north. There were all-purpose stores with fishing gear and warm clothing for people who had forgotten theirs. All the things you needed for being outdoors, really. With cash registers manned by men in their eighties who had only done this: helmed their shops, caught fish, ridden horses, and provided gear for those who wanted to do the same.

When I got to the house I was staying in, just twenty miles from the ranch I had e-mailed my parents about, I was determined to fall in love with the area. I walked up trails from my rental and jumped from boulder to boulder to find the best vantage point from which to see the sprawling valley below. The Owens Valley was famous for having its water stolen to service Los Angeles, just three and a half hours south. What was left were glistening white sheets of saline lakebeds rimmed by snow-capped mountains. I was only a hundred miles from Death Valley and a little over two hundred miles from home, but it felt a world away.

The boulders here were soft-curved from sand and rain, and I leaned back on one of them, staring at the Sierra Mountains, which looked both close and forever away. Through the bright-blue sky careened long threads of spider webs, caught in the light of the waning sunlight. They flew by me one by one, and the place felt magical. I could live here, I thought. *I could disappear here,* I thought. Throughout the sandy and rocky sagebrush terrain were remnants of people. Rocks arranged just so. Rusted cattle fencing that had been knocked over by wind and had begun its slow descent into land, covered by layers of sand, sediment, and slow-growing cacti. It was a predicament I had seen in other places across the desert I had visited in the Southwest. The will of the desert to take the land back from people, to turn it back over to vast nothingness. And yet there was always an endless line of electric poles traversing the expanse, bringing electricity to civilization somewhere.

It was quiet here, so quiet that only the sound of a single bird at a time could be heard. Sometimes a dog bark echoed through the boulders and reached me. And periodically the hum of a fighter jet from a nearby air force base broke the quiet with flight drills. Before the sun set, I walked around the property and found paw prints in the dirt leading up to the house. It could have been a dog or a mountain lion. Beside one print I found a dead mouse. It was black and white and its mouth hung open, its paws suspended in air.

I thought about how my father would answer the questions I asked clients.

"What personal trait have you managed to overcome, Dad?"

"Which day of your life would you like to live over again and why?"

"What brings you joy?"

The answers seemed as impossible to guess as anything Daniel or Daphne or Lawrence would say, and I had known him my entire life.

38.

The town had a bar with wooden saloon doors that conjured images of the Old West. It was a bar like those I had come to find in other desert and mountain towns in California, with wood paneling, and tattered dollar bills stuck to the ceiling and every other possible surface, signed by people who had passed through. People who wanted to leave their mark on this place, to have their notes read, and to be remembered. The stools were Naugahyde—a throwback to another time, just like the booths in Daphne's favorite bar—and taxidermy animal heads punctuated the walls. They had been there so long that each boar head, each buck, had accumulated a layer of dust, and they even had small dust tufts on their whiskers. A shotgun hung above the bar mirror in an overaggressive sign of just what kind of place this was. It was dark and smelled like decades' worth of beer spilled on the floor, but I sat down anyway, and ordered a drink before I could look around and see if anyone else was in the darkened corners with me.

The bartender brought me a beer and shuffled off back to his phone, which was charging in the corner. I looked around and saw a cluster of men in their fifties hovering over the opposite end of the bar. They wore work clothes, and because it wasn't even six o'clock, I assumed this was their first stop before home. I'm not sure what I was looking for exactly—maybe just someone else. I imagined they had come from working the salt flats on the edge of town. I had passed them glistening in the sun on my way in. Their boots were caked in white dust and their faces were the kind of tan you get from spending every day working outside.

I thought about how this side of the Sierras was so different from the Central Valley, just on the other side of the mountains. I had gone there once, late last summer, my first trip there alone. The terrain was much different from the Eastern Sierras, flatter, with smog hanging low over parched fields of yellow. I had hoped that I could find some kind of wilderness as I drove through farmland. The air was thick with smoke, and the entire state had been in the midst of another heat wave—102, 104, 108 degrees, even. Everything felt apocalyptic, like the land was gripped by sickness. And among the signs calling for us to let God re-enter our lives, and testaments of having been saved scrawled on particleboard near driveways that led to small, squat houses, I saw the dead walking alongside the road. They weren't dead, exactly. They just appeared near death: shirtless, methed-out men wandering the roads. Shuffling between the sun-fried grass and road, dirt-hued, with shaved heads. They weren't walking together; instead, they were poking out of the landscape about a mile apart from each other, heading somewhere even they couldn't see.

Driving through those parts of California had made me feel like I was becoming sick, too, so I left and crossed the Sonora Pass to head east, through windy mountain roads where controlled fires were being set. I stopped to watch one as it tore through a vast stretch of trees, and helicopters dropped water down. The air was thick with a smoky fog, and periodically rain would fall through the haze. There was snow in the higher elevations even while everything burned down below. I was above the smoke line, far up in the Sierras, where the deeply packed snow melted down into narrow rivers. I pulled alongside the stretch of road and got out behind other people who had abandoned their cars in order to walk on the snow. Mountain flowers mixed with bright-green grass, and I was glad I'd thrown a winter coat into the trunk of my car before I left.

I watched as people slid around on the snow and felt their joy to have a reprieve from the sickness boiling just down the mountain. It felt like nothing could hurt those of us who had ventured up here. And with no phone service of any kind, nothing could hurt me, either. I didn't have to anticipate a phone call beckoning me to a hospital room, because one wouldn't come if I stayed up there. And so I began seeking out places where I was unreachable.

I sat quietly at the bar and drank as the men around me continued to talk about slights at work. When I paid for my beers and walked outside to the waning light of dusk, no one was on the street, not even hikers leaving the trail to look for somewhere to stay; there was no one to escape into.

39.

All across the West you can find handmade signs begging you to stop for fresh homemade jerky. They are often labeled "the best" or "world's best." I have never stopped for any. At the mouth of the road leading toward Death Valley there is one such sign, connected to a white building that looks like it hasn't been opened in years. I wondered if people stopped and were frequently disappointed.

I had never been to Death Valley, but I remembered that motorcyclist who had turned toward the park on one of my lonely drives. Hoping to see the sunrise over the lowest point in North America, and visit the park before it became unbearably hot, I woke up before dawn. There was one gas station before you turned off, and gas was usually a dollar more per gallon here than anywhere else. Badwater Basin is the point of the lowest elevation in North America, at 282 feet below sea level. Before you even reach the park, you lose phone service.

I passed the salt flats and stared down at the pickup trucks knotted together in a makeshift parking lot. Before I turned right at the intersection that would take me into the valley, I noticed I still had two bars of service. I called Bethanny and left a message.

I said, "Bethanny, it's Evelyn. I'm sorry to be calling out of the blue, but I can't help Daniel. I don't want to help Daniel. I think he'd be better paired with someone like Nathan or even Lorraine. Just not me. Anyone else. I'm sorry."

I drove down a windy two-lane highway past a sixty-six-person town whose decline was directly related to the emptying of the once-full Owens Lake. The leftover houses had the familiar attributes of a mass of bungalows in any number of forgotten desert towns—the kind of place that had once held possibility but now had none. It was on a list of forlorn places, the Bombay Beach of the Eastern Sierras, with yards full of tires, rusted debris that once was useful, strange knickknacks assembled like land art, and houses painted in vivid colors now sun-worn. If you slowed down enough, you could see people stirring inside, though none of them were comfortable being curiosities for the people who passed through.

The cluster of houses edged the vast salt-harvested lands and showed no signs of dying off any further. It was the last stretch of people until you reached Panamint Springs, well within the boundaries of Death Valley.

Inside the park, there were a dozen RVs lined in a row on one side and a restaurant and convenience store on the other. These were the last standing structures you would see for nearly sixty miles of windy roads in a landscape that resembled Mars more than anywhere else on earth. The first hills are covered in black rocks, which give way to mineral-red hills, and finally sherbet-colored mountains. I drove for over an hour through windy terrain, past RVs shepherding families through vacations, couples on road trips, all hoping to catch the sunrise. But I was alone. I stopped on the side of the road to get out of my car and traversed bone-dry cracked-mud terrain. It was completely silent here, and I imagined people before me getting out of their cars and walking into the desert expanse and never looking back. I didn't go far; I was afraid. I needed to pee, but I felt I was too close to the road. The sagebrush was spindly in the way only desert sagebrush could be. I left my driver-side door open on the soft shoulder of the road. Who would take my car out here? Where would they go? The ground was chapped in rounded squares, with layers curling up like chocolate shavings. Nothing lived out here as far as I could tell, though I did see crows perched on signs that spelled out the distance to the next stop or overlook. The park pamphlet had a section on invasive burros. They had been introduced here sometime in the 1880s and had grown in number to ten thousand. But now there were only five hundred left. When I looked at the parched land, I couldn't fathom even that level of desire for survival in days that stretched into 120-degree temperatures.

I found a sand drift, and when I couldn't take it anymore, I pulled down my pants and squatted. I could leave a piece of myself here, mix my DNA with the desert's. I looked up and saw a fighter jet flying low; it flipped up and around, and I wondered if the plane could see me down here. A flash of color among the endless beige.

THE THERAPIST I MISSED the most once told me that people suffer from one of two mental disasters. I loved the term "mental disasters," and said it over and over again when I first heard it. These disasters were the result of profound (or maybe not even) events that happened when we were children, and they felt like a kind of invisible brand that marked us as we moved through the world. They were simple, but dictated elements of